Red-Hot Romeo

(book one of The Royal Romeos series)
by Jenny Gardiner

Copyright © 2016 by Jenny Gardiner

ISBN-13: 978-0983741992
ISBN-10: 0983741999

What people are saying about
Jenny Gardiner's books:

"A fun, sassy read! A cross between Erma Bombeck and Candace Bushnell, reading Jenny Gardiner is like sinking your teeth into a chocolate cupcake...you just want more."

--Meg Cabot, NY Times bestselling author of Princess Diaries, Queen of Babble and more, on Sleeping with Ward Cleaver

"With a strong yet delightfully vulnerable voice, food critic Abbie Jennings embarks on a soulful journey where her love for banana cream pie and disdain for ill-fitting Spanx clash in hilarious and heartbreaking ways. As her body balloons and her personal life crumbles, Abbie must face the pain and secret fears she's held inside for far too long. I cheered for her the entire way."
--Beth Hoffman, NY Times bestselling author of *Saving CeeCee Honeycutt* on *Slim to None*

"Jenny Gardiner has done it again--this fun, fast-paced book is a great summer read."

--Sarah Pekkanen, NY Times bestselling author of *The Opposite of Me*, on *Slim to None*

"As Sweet as a song and sharp as a beak, *Bite Me* really soars as a memoir about family--children and husbands, feathers and fur--and our capacity to keep loving though life may occasionally bite."

--Wade Rouse, bestselling author of At Least in the City Someone Would Hear Me Scream

Chapter One

ALESSANDRO Romeo was sipping his Negroni on the rocks, enjoying a beautiful sunset on the terrace of his winery's palazzo that overlooked his family's vast estate, when he noticed a fat curl of dark smoke trailing skyward on the other side of the sprawling Tuscan manor home. Quickly setting his drink aside, he raced down the terrace steps, rushed through a gauntlet of tall, narrow cypress trees, and across the Italian garden in front of the palazzo as the acrid smell of smoke grew stronger and black clouds of it enveloped more of the once-melon-colored, late-day sky.

In the distance, he spotted a tiny white sports car racing down the estate's long, cypress-lined driveway just as he finally came upon the source of the now-choking smoke: his beloved Lamborghini Aventador Superveloce— a cool half million dollars of premier driving pleasure— sizzling away with the crackle of fire and lick of flames that were embracing his dream car and turning it into a veritable conflagration.

"*Aiuto!*" Sandro shouted, calling for the farmhands to help, if not to salvage his burning car, then at least to keep the vehicle from exploding and injuring someone. "Help! Bring water, *prontissimo!*"

The *Cantine dei Marchesi Romeo* was a vineyard with many employees still working into late afternoon in the fields, so within a minute several workers had arrived, directing hoses and buckets of water to douse the fire until

1

all that was left were the charred remains of his beloved sports car. Sandro felt grateful that at least they'd stopped the fire before it spread.

"*Vaffanculo, si strega*," Sandro said, shaking his fist in rage toward the now-long-departed car he'd seen racing away from the scene. *Fuck off, you witch*. It didn't take much to deduce who'd torched the thing: he'd just seen the taillights of his hot-tempered, on-again/off-again girlfriend Gia Sandretti's convertible trailing down the long drive. The woman had already resorted to plenty of other extreme ways to express her irrational jealous rages, including recently impaling him with the heel of one of her Manolo Blahniks—which resulted in five stitches to his arm—so he knew immediately that this bore her telltale fingerprints.

He'd tried to extricate himself from the relationship more times than he could count at this point; it hadn't been but a few months into dating her that he knew she had a streak of green running through her like a river of toxic waste. Alessandro couldn't so much as inadvertently glance at another woman, even in a magazine, without Gia flipping out on him, which meant the usual stream of foul language spewed at him alongside crazed accusations and the occasional hurled glass object or other breakable.

By nature a genial and fun-loving guy, he'd put up with it, thinking that eventually she'd find her way to another man to harass, but as much as he'd tried to let her go gently so as not to trigger her impetuous fury, she simple wasn't getting the hint.

Sure Gia, a stunningly statuesque brunette, was gorgeous, but he hadn't taken to calling her Crazy Gia for nothing. And the last thing Sandro needed in his life was a drama-queen fashion model with no self-control who acted more like a secret police interrogator than a lover.

Sandro had met Gia at one of the many social functions he normally attended as principle of the world-famous Cantine dei Marchesi Romeo winemakers. His was an Italian family with a history of six hundred years of wine-making and roots that reached back to the days of Italian nobility and the famed house of Savoy. His family had immediate ties to the royals of neighboring Monaforte as well, as his uncle Enrico, Duke of Santo Miele, was married to that country's Queen Ariana.

Officially Alessandro's title was Marchese Alessandro Romeo, but he tended to downplay that archaic terminology except when necessary at official events where the cachet of the royal title helped with his family business. Or as was more often the case in the past, when it helped him pick up beautiful women.

No doubt it's what had drawn Gia to him in the first place, aside from his handsome good looks. He wore his thick, wavy dark hair to near his shoulders, often pulled back in a ponytail, and sported a neatly trimmed goatee and moustache that proved irresistible to many women. His sincere brown eyes caused them to swoon even more. Throw in a royal title, a famous family name, and plenty of wealth, and Sandro was delicious catnip that most women simply couldn't resist. Except when it came to nutters like Gia, who seemed to want to push him away, all while clinging desperately to him as if he were a gangrenous appendage. But this was the last straw with her; this time he would file a police complaint and ensure that she was no longer allowed anywhere near him nor could she have anything to do with him. Enough was enough.

Six weeks later...

Sandro dusted off his hands and placed them on his hips, beaming as he gazed at the object of his near-undivided attention for the past six years: the design and building of a massive new headquarters, a place that would house the offices of Marchesi Romeo wines but also become a tourist destination for wine lovers the world over. It had been Sandro's dream to create this destination venue, something he'd imagined for several years prior to actually implementing the plan.

He and his family had collaborated with one of the top Italian architects to envision the one-of-a-kind design of the building, constructed with local materials, intended to keep in harmony with the landscape while remaining environmentally friendly, energy efficient, and ultimately to serve as a veritable work of art in the Tuscan countryside. And in a few days, others would finally be able to share in Sandro's dream come true at the grand-opening gala. Guests who would attend included celebrities, political leaders, prominent local officials, and of course family and friends.

Sandro had reached out to his favorite cousin, Luca, the youngest of the Monaforte princes, to ensure his attendance. Monaforte was a small European principality on the Mediterranean with strong ties to Italy.

"You know I'll disown you if you don't show up," Sandro said, teasing his dearest friend. "I'll cut off your vino supply—hit you where it'll hurt most."

Luca had for a long time been Sandro's social sidekick but last year had settled into a relationship with a European-based American reporter named Larkin Mallory, and now it was as if he barely left the comfort of his living room. Sandro hated how complacent men became once they got "whipped": always at the woman's beck and call, never free to do as they pleased.

Now that Gia was out of the picture, he was going to make sure he didn't allow a woman to cloud his judgment and create hassles for him ever again. *No thank you.* The loss of his expensive sports car was a small price to pay to learn that lesson.

"I'd be crazy not to show up at this one," Luca said. "It's the event of the season, I hear. Even homebodies like me will be there."

"Homebodies," his cousin said with a grumble. "Whatever happened to the man I knew who partied till dawn and couldn't be bothered with such things as commitment?"

Luca laughed. "You know that was ninety percent urban legend anyhow. It's not like I really caroused that much."

"Yeah, well, sometimes the legend is as true as fact."

"That's what's wrong with this world."

"You've become a grumpy old man."

"Not grumpy. Happily settled is all," Luca said. "You should give it a try sometime. No more out on the prowl, hoping to get laid without catching any communicable diseases. It's a good thing."

"Hell no," Sandro said. "You do know about Gia's latest—and final—batshit-crazy maneuver?"

"Of course," Luca said. "I always suspected there was something off about that one. Even when you first started dating, she was irrationally demanding. Like when you dragged me to that godforsaken fashion show she was in just so she would have an audience."

"Tell me about it," he said. "Yet one more reason I will never cross paths with a fashion model again. Ever. Those women are the worst. I think they get hangry from lack of food and go totally *pazzo*."

"Hangry?"

"It's a combination of hungry and angry," he said. "All the worse for Gia because she's an Italian girl who can't eat pasta. *Mamma mia*, what kind of life is that? Who wouldn't be crazy-like?"

"Well, in that case I'd better apologize in advance because Larkin is bringing along her friend Taylor to your gala and, well…" He lowered his voice to a whisper. "She's a fashion model."

Sandro shook his head even though Luca couldn't see him. "No, thank you. I'll take a pass. You can have her all to yourself. If that's your thing."

"If what's my thing?"

"If you want to hook up with her."

"Are you crazy? I'm perfectly happy with Larkin. Not looking to add anyone into the relationship," he said. "I was thinking maybe you'd like Taylor. She's beautiful, of course. But she's really sweet as well. Completely down-to-earth."

"No. Models. Ever, dude," he said. "Ever."

"Be my guest. Go ahead and punish yourself," Luca said. "But I think you'll regret it. You'd be lucky if she'd have anything to do with you anyhow."

"No doubt," Sandro said. "But do me a favor, just keep her far, far from me. I want no part of any of those crazy women, and this is a night I intend to completely avoid erratic females with bad tempers. So whatever you do, spare me."

"Fine," he said. "I'll respect your wishes. But don't get mad at me when I say I told you so."

"To the contrary, *mio cugino*, it's for the best," Sandro said even though his curiosity was already getting the best of him as he Googled supermodels named Taylor to see exactly what she looked like. Old habits, after all, were hard to break.

Chapter Two

NOTHING *like a good black-tie party,* Taylor McFarland thought, taking a final sip of champagne as her plane made its final approach in Florence. She'd get to dress in yet another amazing designer gown, and hot men in tuxedos would be plentiful. It was so up her alley. It was why she was on her way to Italy, and this one promised to be particularly fabulous—a spectacular venue in an architecturally creative structure built into the hillside at some Italian guy's vineyard. And the wine would be flowing freely.

What's not to love? Plus she was joining her good friend Larkin and Larkin's boyfriend Luca, and she always had fun with the two of them. Talk about opposites attracting: Larkin had been such a quiet little mouse of a woman when they first met, and Luca, well, he was a prince, a bit of a bon vivant, and used to the limelight. It was lovely that the two of them had found each other, albeit after some struggles. Taylor had helped to spruce up Larkin's appearance a bit, steering her away from the clothing-as-camouflage manner of dress, and Larkin had taken to it with a vengeance, had now practically achieved Taylor's level of clothing obsession.

Luca had invited Taylor to join them and to stay at the palazzo owned by his winemaker cousin whose vineyard supposedly made one of the most famous wines in Tuscany. Luca had promised her he was a lot of fun, but Taylor wasn't on the prowl anyhow. She was over dealing with men who were nothing but a pain in her butt, thank you. She was perfectly happy to just go and browse the merchandise without making a purchase. Besides, she didn't have time for dalliances right now; she had much more important things to do than have to tag-team a long-distance relationship.

Taylor had recently started a charitable organization called Rags to Riches to help children who couldn't afford to buy clothes piece together outfits that would allow them to not feel like outsiders. Having grown up in a household with a single mother who struggled to pay the bills each month, Taylor knew what it was like to show up to school in the same threadbare outfits all the time: it was demoralizing, and kids loved to taunt the ones who looked like they'd just come in off the streets.

If she had a dollar for every time kids called her white trash, she'd have had plenty of money to clothe herself as she was able to now that she had become a famous *fashionista*. So it was particularly gratifying to be able to help out other children. It might seem like a superficial thing, providing decent clothes to a kid, but having come from those very circumstances of lacking, she totally got what it meant to them and knew that even a little bit of window dressing could make a difference.

She figured a lot of powerful people with money would be in attendance at this event, and they were her favorite type to strong-arm into making fabulous donations. A Christie Brinkley look-alike with gentle, sun-bleached blond waves and soft blue eyes, the American supermodel was not beyond using her looks and stature to get what she wanted if it helped others in need. She knew wealthy men in particular would never turn down a

gorgeous woman in a slinky evening gown soliciting them for funds. Which made her happy just as long as they didn't presume she was soliciting anything else.

After a smooth landing, Taylor was off the plane quickly and through customs in no time at all. As she exited the security area with her luggage, she saw Larkin and Luca practically entwined on a bench near the entryway, oblivious to her existence while they made out like a couple of horny teenagers.

She wheeled her bag up to them and cleared her throat. "Ahem," she said, crossing her arms and tapping her toe, staring at them both, her brow arched.

Larkin detached quickly and blushed. "Oh, Taylor! So sorry! Luca and I were just, uh, getting reacquainted after being apart for a few minutes while I ran to the restroom."

Larkin grinned as her boyfriend swiped his finger along her lips to remove some excess saliva. Gross. Her friend stood up and gave Taylor a warm embrace.

"Please," Taylor said, shaking her head as she hugged her friend. "I'm totally used to PDA when I'm around you two. I would have expected nothing less. I'm just impressed you kept your clothes on."

Larkin gave her a playful smack.

It did make her laugh how Larkin had gone from such a wallflower to a bit of a wild child. It was nice to see her come into her own.

"I was merely expressing my affection for Luca like any true Italian would."

"Only you're not Italian."

"When in Rome then?" Larkin grinned.

"We're in Florence. Duh," Taylor said.

"It doesn't matter," Luca reached for Larkin's hand.

"Soon she'll be an official member of the Monaforte royal family. And that means she'll technically even have some Italian ties, being that my father is one hundred percent hot-blooded Italian. She'll practically be Italian herself." He winked.

"Oh my God!" Taylor said with a squeal, pulling Larkin into a hug. "You two are getting married? What? When? How? And I won't ask why, because, well, that's obvious." She grabbed Larkin's left hand and lifted it up to inspect the three-stone crown-set ring with a center ruby surrounded by old European-cut diamonds.

"It's from Monaforte's crown jewel collection," Luca said. "I consulted with my mother before choosing it, but it belonged to the only other blond member of the royal family, a very distant great-great-great-grandmother or something. Mum thought it would be fitting for Larkin to have this ring."

"It's stunning, Larks," Taylor said, holding her hands up to her face in surprise. "I'm just so overwhelmed about this! But I want to know all the details!"

"So we'd just spent a few days in Venice," she said. "On the last evening, before a breathtaking sunset on the Grand Canal in front of the *Piazza San Marco*, we were being serenaded by our gondolier when Luca got down on one knee and asked for my hand!"

"I can't even believe it," Taylor said. "Fairy-tale perfect. Wow. I'm so glad there are still romantic men in the world. I was starting to think they all died in the Pleistocene era."

Luca laughed, scrubbing his hands in his hair. "Were there humans back then? Or were we still mollusks?"

Taylor rolled her eyes. "I think humans were just

getting started then. Nothing personal, but men are still mollusks if you ask me."

He gave her two thumbs-up. "Thanks for that vote of confidence."

"Aww, poor Taylor has plenty of reason to be sour on men," Larkin said, squeezing her friend's hand. "What's it been, like five guys in a row who ended up only wanting to be with you because you're a model? And when they found out you actually did things with your life other than look beautiful and decorate their arms, they walked away? I think the problem is you've got to find the right man and not the troglodytes you've been dating."

"Yeah, no more men who want to drag me by the hair back to the cave so I can prepare a fat brontosaurus steak for him."

"I don't know about you, but all this talk of prehistory is making me hungry," Luca said, rubbing his stomach. "In fact, a good, bloody Florentine steak sounds awesome."

"I'm with you," Taylor said. "I had just enough champagne on the plane to remind me I haven't eaten since my measly croissant at breakfast."

"Perfect," Larkin said. "We've got reservations for dinner in Florence, and we'll drive down to Sandro's afterward."

Taylor scrunched her nose. "Speaking of troglodytes. I know you guys want to fix me up with him, but really, I am so not interested."

"Oh stop," Larkin said, waving her hand dismissively. "He's a really sweet guy once you get to know him. I thought he was a jerk at first too, but honestly, I think you'll like him."

"Wow. There's a ringing endorsement," Taylor said,

arching her brow. "At any rate, you're sure it's okay with my tagging along? I mean I'm happy to come to this big fête, but I don't want to be an imposition."

"First off, you, my dear, would never be an imposition," Luca said. "Secondly, my cousin Alessandro won't even know you're there, the place is that big. It's a palace, literally. A gigantic Renaissance palazzo. It could be days until he knows if any of us are there. Plus I'm sure he's going to be at the new building overseeing the finishing touches. So no worries."

Taylor shrugged. "Okay, if you're sure. I'd just hate to have the man be mad that I'm invading his space."

Luca shook his head. "Not at all. Besides, he's always had a thing for models."

Taylor shook her head. Yet one more reason she would have exactly nothing to do with him.

Chapter Three

IT was well after midnight when Sandro heard the crunch of tires on the pebbled driveway. That was the thing about living in the rural countryside: you inevitably picked up the slightest sounds late at night, so not much got past Sandro. It's why he still kicked himself that he hadn't heard Crazy Gia barreling up the driveway when she came to destroy his beloved car.

Ahhh… Gia… The only good thing about what happened with her was finally casting the woman from his life once and for all. That at least afforded him the chance to focus on important things, like overseeing the many finishing touches on his baby, his labor of love; the time was finally upon him to share it with the world, so it was essential he not be distracted with her nonsense.

The bad news of course was his car was a total loss. As was their relationship, though victory was perhaps a more appropriate description of the fallout: he was more than happy to have a restraining order taken out against the woman, which meant finally he could be done with her hotheaded reprisals, most of which were rooted in her own fantasy world of unfounded mistrust. The security guards had changed the passcode on the entrance gate to the palazzo, and unless Gia wanted to trek through the dense woods in the steep Chianti hillside surrounding his property to try to get back at him again, she was out of luck. Hopefully she'd move on to haunt some other poor sucker. And now, with his lesson well learned, Sandro had called it quits on women for a while; they weren't worth the hassle, and he had the stiletto scar and the charred vehicle to prove it.

As the tires on gravel came to a stop, he heard the chatter of voices out front and then car doors slamming and knew it had to be Luca and company, so he shut down his computer at his desk, closed off the lights in his office, and hastened down the hall to greet his houseguests. The staff was off at this hour, and the rest of the household had long since retreated to bed; each of his brothers occupied a wing of the palazzo. They had complete autonomy and could choose whether to be together or on their own throughout the course of the day. Each of them took on different duties in the running of the company, so there was little stepping on toes since they all enjoyed complete independence over day-to-day issues.

Sandro stepped onto the open-air loggia at the front of the house just as his guests arrived.

"Ciao, Luca," he said, reaching his arms out and embracing his friend as he kissed his cheeks and asked how he was doing. "*Come va?*"

"*Benissimo, grazie*," Luca said. "I'm great, thank you. And you remember Larkin?" He extended his arm toward her.

"Of course," Sandro said. "The most beautiful Larkin, looking stellar as usual." They exchanged a two-cheek kiss.

"And this is Larkin's good friend Taylor," Luca said. "Taylor, I'd like you to meet my cousin Alessandro."

"*Piacere*," Taylor said, telling him she was pleased to meet him. "Thank you so much for your hospitality."

Sandro extended his hand to shake hers just as she reached out to kiss his cheeks, and what resulted was a

completely awkward greeting that left her blushing and him wondering what it was with American women that they couldn't read up on protocol when in a different country.

Luca and Larkin laughed to offset the awkwardness of the moment, but they then all stood in silence for a moment.

Taylor broke the uncomfortable quiet by reaching for a gift she'd forgotten to hand to him when they were introduced. "I was just in France, and well, when in Paris…"

Sandro untied the large silver bow and pulled a bottle of Bordeaux from the package. He looked at the bottle for a minute, not sure if it was a serious gift or a joke of some sort. Because who would bring a gift of wine to a man who oversaw one of Tuscany's premier wine empires? No doubt it was a perfectly fine bottle of wine, but still… It wasn't anywhere near as good as his own, of that he felt certain.

"Ahhh. Vino. *Grazie mille*," he said, staring at the label. "I'm sure we'll enjoy this." He cocked his brow, and Luca threw him the side eye.

"I'm sure Taylor thought a wine connoisseur such as yourself always likes to sample the competition."

"But of course," Sandro said, rubbing his beard as a distraction. He was a little tripped up with the arrival of Larkin's friend because it was as if a strong wind had momentarily blown away his bad feelings toward the fairer sex, ushering in a gentle and soothing sea breeze; she was that breathtakingly beautiful. She was tall, with endless legs he couldn't stop staring at, and soft, wavy blond hair. Her eyes were the shade of azure you might encounter along the shores of the Amalfi Coast—the type of water that lures you against your better judgment to take just a tiny dip. She was like no woman he'd ever encountered before. Yet he knew even then the chances of the water being an agreeable temperature were not so great, and beneath the surface, who knew what dangerous creatures loomed? His gut reminded him he was far wiser to avoid the potential risk to life and limb. Worse yet take a chance of diving into too-shallow water and breaking his neck.

Beauty was no longer going to be that demanding football coach that would bark commands at his subservient cock. No way. Beauty had gotten him into deep trouble with Crazy Gia, so he was going to hang up his figurative cleats, which meant ignoring the siren call of a gorgeous woman for his own sanity, not to mention the sake of his replacement car.

"So," Luca said, rubbing his hands together as Taylor strolled along the loggia, inspecting the ancient statues that graced the terrace-like area. "We had a great meal in *Firenze*, just me and my fiancée and her best friend." His face broke into a large grin as Larkin held up her left hand, wiggling her ring finger so that Sandro would notice.

His cousin knit his brow. "Surely I didn't hear what I thought I just heard."

Luca nodded. "It's true, my friend. Your cousin has fallen hard. Looks like it's your turn next."

Sandro held his hands up in false surrender. "Are you completely *pazzo*? You must be crazy to think I would ever fall prey to such a disease."

Larkin frowned. "Wait a minute. I'm not sure if I should be insulted by that comment."

"I think the polite thing to do would be to extend your heartfelt congratulations and then keep your mouth shut," Taylor said, throwing Sandro some shade as she stood up

for her friend.

Sandro's brow furrowed deep enough to plant a row of grapevines in. "I beg your pardon?"

"As well you should," she said, half glaring at him.

"My comments had nothing to do with these two lovebirds," he said, placing a hand on each of their shoulders. "But rather are simply a reflection of my own wishes."

"That's fine if you aren't interested in being married," Taylor said. "But you came across as disapproving of them, and I don't want you creating a rift between 'these two lovebirds' with your insensitivity."

"My insensitivity?"

"If the shoe fits."

Luca raised his hands. "Children," he said, clapping his hands to get them in line. "We're going to have to break up this schoolyard brawl. It's late, and I know if I don't get eight hours of sleep, well, I'm going to be a bear in the morning."

"It's okay, you can be my cozy bear," Larkin said as she reached for his hand, which made Sandro about gag.

"*Mio cugino*," Sandro said. "My cousin. I didn't mean to insult anyone. Let's first toast your wonderful news with our private cellar reserve grappa. I don't take this out for just anyone."

He led them inside to a private study with a small bar, then pulled out four glasses and poured the light amber liquid. He handed a glass to each of his guests.

"*Salute e benessere*," he said, nodding to Luca and Larkin. "To the happy couple: to health and wellness."

"*Cin cin*," Luca said, tipping his glass to Larkin's, then Taylor's.

"As you know, to be a winemaker is to be a risk taker, yet also to know great patience," Sandro said. "It sounds much like the role of a husband." He laughed, and Luca joined with him. Larkin smiled a tepid smile, the type women make if someone asks when the due date is when they're actually just overweight. Not a smile with sincerity behind it but rather more of a cringe. Taylor, on the other hand, grimaced.

Larkin leaned over and whispered in her friend's ear. "So maybe I was wrong that you and Alessandro would hit it off," she said. "But you're here now, so please don't worry about defending my honor. I'm totally fine, and I really don't want to make waves. Just roll with it, okay?"

Taylor heaved a sigh. "Fine. But if he keeps up with the insults, he might just find himself on the receiving end of my wrath. And I'm pretty sure he would live to regret that."

Luca leaned in to speak in hushed tones with his cousin. "I see you've not gotten past the whole Gia episode then?"

He growled. "Gotten past? It's hardly been two months. I haven't even had a chance to tackle my insurance claims on the car, let alone deal with the emotional fallout."

Luca lifted an eyebrow. "Emotional fallout? Who are you fooling? You didn't care much for Gia for a long time. I'm pretty sure the emotional fallout ends in a Euro sign and is all about your car."

He shrugged. "Yeah, so, okay. I wasn't all that bereft when it ended. Finally." One side of his mouth lifted in an impish grin.

"So then why the cranky behavior?" Luca said. "You're not making a good first impression on our guest."

Sandro shook his head. "I want to make it abundantly clear that I am off-limits to your guest and to any other female who might happen into my little space in the world. I don't want her—or any woman, for that matter—to mistake me for someone who cares."

"Ouch," Luca said. "You're sounding a bit bitter."

Sandro rubbed his hands together, then lifted them into the air as if in defeat. "Maybe," he said, running his hands through his hair. "More like weary. Weary of all the nonsense I went through with Gia, but also just tired. I suppose I've been so bowled over with this big project. I'm working too hard, not sleeping enough—"

"Not getting laid," Luca said. "I know you, Sandro. You're cranky because you're not getting any."

"Oh stop," he said. "It's why God gave us hands."

Luca laughed out loud, causing both the women to look at him. "A poor substitute, as you well know."

"Maybe so, but my motto is any port in a storm," Sandro said. "For now I'll settle for a poor substitute, which at least won't make *me* poor by destroying the next four-hundred-thousand-euro car I get."

Luca playfully shoved his cousin. "Fine," he said, waving his hands to dismiss him. "Be stubborn. But I sure don't know why you'd settle for a box of dried raisins when you have a bunch of lush, lovely grapes hanging right in front of you, ripe for the picking if you played your cards right."

Sandro rolled his eyes. "By that I assume you're not suggesting I go make love to my grapevines but rather pursue her?" He nodded his head toward Taylor.

"Uh, that might get pretty uncomfortable, what with all those sharp stick things poking off them," Luca said.

"But if I were you, I'd pluck the low-hanging fruit that's dangling right before your eyes. And maybe then the two of you could make love amidst your grapevines if you really wanted to incorporate that into your sexual experience. After all, you're an Italian man. Hardly one to shy away from a little fun. Try it, you might like it."

"I might like to have my balls waxed bare with hot paraffin too, but I highly doubt it," he said, turning to the women. "On that note, I think it's time to retire, my friends. I'll show you to your rooms and wish you a *buona notte.*"

Chapter Four

TAYLOR had been looking forward to arriving at Luca's cousin's vineyard. After all, a weekend at a beautiful retreat in the heart of Italy's wine country sounded like the perfect way to spend some downtime.

After a long stroll through Florence and an amazing four-course meal on a small rooftop terrace overlooking the Arno River, she enjoyed the scenic ride to Sandro's in Luca's charcoal-gray Alfa Romeo Giulia, fighting sleep the whole way. It had been a long day, and she was ready to settle down for the night. After arriving at Sandro's palatial estate, they got out of the car and Taylor just stood for a moment, her senses alive with the sights and sounds of this beautiful countryside. She'd traveled the world enough to know that Tuscany was one of her happy places. Aside from the food, the wine, and the people, the inherent beauty and serenity of the countryside really spoke to her and soothed her soul.

Cooler night air had slipped in unannounced, and she rubbed her bare arms against the slight chill as she focused her attention on the chorus of emerging cicadas, the croak of tree frogs, the call of blackbirds, and the rustle of leaves in the night breeze as if transfixed by a beautiful symphony. The inky sky was aglow with twinkling fireflies, and the place felt downright magical.

"So this is it," Luca said, spreading his arms. "Not a bad place to spend the weekend, right?"

Taylor shrugged. "Beats sleeping on the streets." She

smiled to herself, considering that during her childhood there had been times when she was a little too close to that reality for comfort. "It's absolutely perfect, Luca. Thanks so much for inviting me. I think it will be an amazing weekend."

The perfume of roses hung heavy in the air, and as she passed several rosebushes, Taylor bent down to breathe in the aroma, aware of the lone hoot of an owl in the distance. "I think I'm going to love this place."

She'd taken her shoes off in the car and carried them as she climbed the staircase toward the open-air loggia. The warmth of the terra-cotta tile warmed her feet, and she felt as one with the place, as if she belonged there. It was a shame the feeling didn't last long, because once she met Luca's arrogant cousin, she couldn't help but think she wanted to get far, far away from him and anything to do with him. She'd have been in the first Uber out of the place were that an option. Unfortunately, she didn't think she even had a cell signal, let alone Uber service, out here.

She resolved to accept her fate for the next few days as she was to be a guest of a man clearly taken by his own self-importance, one she'd rather give a swift kick in the shins than a kiss on the lips. And when he'd started making acerbic remarks about Luca and Larkin's engagement, she had to clench her fists to her sides to not reach out and smack him one just to shut him up. She worried maybe he'd poisoned the grappa he shared with them in the celebratory toast to the happy couple just to keep them from marrying, he was so cynical about women and relationships in general. What a buzzkill. Oh well, she wasn't going to let his bad mood impact her temperament.

The jovial little drinks celebration couldn't have ended

soon enough, so she was thrilled when he announced he was going to show them all to their rooms.

"If you just point the way, I'm sure I can find it," Taylor said, hoping to get away from Sandro before she was forced to feed him more of her mind.

"That won't be possible," he said.

She knit her brows. "Anything's possible. Try me. I've got a good sense of direction. I promise you won't have to send out a search party."

"Why don't Sandro and I grab the bags and you girls wait here for us," Luca said, his idea a little pickax breaking the ice in the room.

"Don't worry, Luca. I'm perfectly happy to get my own suitcase," Taylor said. "You don't need to do that."

Sandro frowned and held his hand out as she tried to follow them down the steps to Luca's car. "Stay there. I've got it."

Taylor rolled her eyes behind his back. "Where'd you find that loser?" she asked her friend.

"Stop," Larkin said. "He's really not usually like this. I don't know what's gotten into him."

"I think a bloated ego is it."

"Really, he's normally very nice."

"If this is nice, I'd hate to see him behaving badly."

"Well," Larkin said. "Looks like you two are destined for happiness together." She laughed.

"Honestly," Taylor said. "What a crank he is. I'd no sooner consider even a brief fling with him than I'd contemplate a one-way ticket to Mars."

"Nothing personal, but I think the feeling might be mutual," a deep voice behind her said.

Taylor looked over her shoulder to see her host

standing there, her suitcase in one of his hands, her garment bag in the other. He had a half grin on his face, and she wasn't sure if that meant he was trying to be funny or he was just enjoying busting her making a rude remark about him.

"Oh, um, uh," Taylor said. As much as she was unimpressed with the man, she didn't want him to know she thought he was a rude git.

"Luca," Sandro said, not dwelling on their unpleasant exchange. "You two will stay in the usual place. I'll show your friend Princess Charming to her room." He smirked at her.

Great. Now not only was the man a complete jerk, but on top of it all he also knew that she thought he was. She was just going to have to resign herself to making the most of this weekend and at least trying to leverage this party to raise funds for her charity. At least then something good would come of it.

Chapter Five

WHAT a sassy thing she was, Sandro thought as he overheard her busting his balls. Here he thought he'd figured that one out already, pegging her as the typical clothes-obsessed, status-oriented *me! me! me!* fashion-model type. And maybe she was that. But she had a little spark to her—albeit a combustible one—which was, he really hated to admit it, intriguing as hell. He sort of liked it when someone gave him shit, especially when he deserved it.

He knew he'd been a complete prick tonight; he somehow just couldn't help himself. What was he thinking, embarrassing poor Larkin like that? Just because his relationships had led to trouble didn't mean that Luca and Larkin wouldn't be perfectly happy together. Statistically unlikely, but, well, stranger things had happened in the world.

He wasn't sure why the idea of them pairing up for all eternity bothered him so much. Was it because she was taking his playmate away from him for good? Even he knew that was completely childish. He was a grown man—he couldn't carouse like a twenty-year-old forever. Not that he even got to carouse when he was twenty—maybe that was the real issue with him. But wasn't he allowed to be at least a little bit possessive about this? He and Luca had been friends far longer than Luca had been in love with Larkin. And yet here he'd been instantly supplanted by the woman. It sort of sucked.

Damn, it was downright surprising what a good

shagging could lead to. At least he assumed that was what was behind his engagement—why else would the man give up his freedom if it weren't for an amazing lay? Though even Sandro wouldn't yield in that regard. He'd had plenty of mind-blowing sex before, yet never was it worth abandoning your freedom forever. *Hell no!* Life was too short for that sacrifice. He might as well skewer himself on a spit and be left on the altar as a sacrifice to the gods.

In the meantime, he was stuck being a polite host to this feisty thing he couldn't help but be a little bit curious about, even as he wished he could send her back to wherever she came from before he did something really stupid like listen to his damned libido that was telling him to take advantage of her proximity. Christ, it had been too long since he'd had proper sex. He was going to have to take matters into his own hands as it were, just as soon as he showed her to her room. Otherwise, he was going to be on tenterhooks the whole bloody weekend.

They walked down a long, dark corridor overflowing with antique busts, statues, and paintings. Sandro always felt reassured when wandering the hallways of this vast palazzo: these were his people surrounding him, his history embracing him every waking moment. His successes rested on the shoulders of so many generations before him, and he felt enormous pressure not just to maintain but to exceed his ancestors' impressive achievements in order to ensure that Romeo wines remained the best in all of Italy.

"I'm really perfectly capable of carrying my own things," Taylor said, trying to relieve him of her garment bag, but Sandro pulled it out of her reach.

"Wouldn't hear of it," he said. "What sort of gentleman would I be then?"

She threw him a sidelong glance. "Uh, maybe you didn't get the memo."

He let out a laugh. "Right. So far you've been unimpressed with my manners. That's okay. I get that. You need to understand that Luca and I go way back, and I can say things to him that perhaps are inappropriate for the tender ears of outsiders."

She remained silent, but he could see she was glaring again.

"What?" he said. "What did I say now?"

"It's sort of rude to suggest that I'm not a friend of Luca and Larkin's," she said. "I might not be the almighty BFF to Luca that you are, but I'm hardly an 'outsider.'" She made demonstrative air quotes to drive home her point.

He stopped for a moment and held up his hands in surrender. "Fine," he said. "No harm meant. I was just speaking off the cuff. I didn't realize I had to have my speech vetted before you could hear any of it."

Her eyes grew wide. "I think you'd better just quit before you do something crazy, like put your foot in your mouth. Oh, too late. You already did that." She snatched her garment bag from his hands and quickly walked ahead of him.

"Feel free to lead the way, but you haven't a clue where you're headed."

She slowed down and let him pass her with a grimace on her face. Clearly she had no plans to walk alongside him.

"I hope you don't mind your room not being near your friend. Luca always stays in the same room when he visits—he even keeps spare supplies there so he doesn't have to carry them with him," he said. "Besides, I thought I'd put you up in a room that overlooks the valley below.

The sunrise is spectacular here—if you can get up early enough to witness it."

"I'll be sure to set my alarm."

Damn, she sure sounded like she was being a smart-ass there.

"The only downside is you're across the hall from me. Which I'm sure won't be a problem for you as I can assure you I won't bother you at all. At any rate, breakfast is served on the terrace until nine," he said. "And no doubt with your innate tracking skills, you'll be able to find your way there without any problems."

She smirked at him. "I think I can follow the smell, thanks."

"In that case, we've arrived at your room. I hope you have a comfortable night's sleep."

He opened the door, set her suitcase on an antique luggage rack, and dipped in a sarcastic bow as he left the room without another word. The last thing he wanted to do was spend even a minute more in that woman's presence considering the state of sexual desperation he was currently in and the fact that he found her far more intriguing on so many levels than he'd ever care to admit.

Chapter Six

WHEN they reached a gilded door and Sandro stopped, turned the knob, and opened the door to the most beautiful room she'd ever seen, she could barely believe it. Sometimes she still had to pinch herself to realize how far she'd come. There had been a time when she was lucky to sleep in the backseat of her mother's rusted-out Ford Taurus, when they were so poor they had no home and no beds to sleep in.

Ever since she'd become a famous model and could rest her head anywhere she wanted to, she made sure she covered the windows against any early-morning sun: it tended to give her flashbacks to her childhood, waking with the sun streaming into the car windows. Back then, the only good thing about dawn was realizing they'd passed the night safely. So the idea of having those curtains open to see the sunrise was so not something she would consider. The biggest luxury she could imagine for a long time was installing blackout shades in the home she'd purchased for her mother. She relished her privacy and the ability to sleep until she woke rather than until the day broke, and on those rare occasions that she'd get home, she wanted to sleep until she could sleep no more.

She stood and gazed in awe at the room. She was spoiled—she'd stayed in luxurious hotels all over the world. But this room exceeded the most exclusive hotels in which she'd been a guest. It was one step away from something you'd see at Versailles; it was that opulent.

Draped across the oversized king mahogany bed was a sumptuous, rich, deep blue velvet down-filled comforter surrounded by piles of pillows. The curtains hadn't been drawn along a wall of windows, so greeting her was the star-filled sky she'd savored an hour earlier. She stared outside, the terrain beginning to take shape as her eyes adjusted to the darkness below, and with what little light the tiny sliver of moon afforded, she could just make out the undulating hills planted full of grapevines as far as the eye could see.

A gilded chandelier was suspended from the ceiling, and the walls were covered in a softer shade of blue damask. The headboard of hand-carved mahogany was trimmed in gilt, and coordinating blue velvet was suspended from a canopy, enveloping the bed in private comfort. She could get used to living in this room. If only it didn't involve the existence of that unpleasant cousin of Luca's. Strange, Luca and his family all seemed so lovely; that man must be from the black sheep side of the family.

After Taylor unpacked her belongings and hung up her clothes in the matching antique wardrobe, she got ready for bed. She stood before that wall of windows as she brushed her teeth, just staring into the dark night sky, feeling totally at peace. A shooting star streaked across the cobalt sky, and she made a wish on it. It's not as if most of Taylor's wishes hadn't already been answered; she was fortunate enough to have overcome a rough beginning to now live an enviable lifestyle. She was one of the lucky ones. But she knew there were many children even less fortunate than she had been, and she wanted them to be able to enjoy the riches of life too. Was that asking too much?

Just before bed, Taylor pulled back the comforter and

returned to the windows to draw the curtains tightly closed.
Yet for some reason she couldn't do it: the blanket of stars
that studded the sky was so beautiful. And that shooting
star. Maybe she could stare into the distance and see
another one. She knew she felt safest with protection from
the outside, so it would take a lot for her to resist the need
to pull the heavy velvet draperies closed. But she was
perfectly safe, two floors up, in the middle of the
countryside. She was no longer a small child in the back of
an old car, parked near a bridge underpass where the police
wouldn't make her mother move the car in the middle of
the night. Out of sight, out of mind was how her mother
viewed it. But Taylor always felt perfectly exposed to prying
eyes, vulnerable to the creatures of the night.

She lay in silence, secure beneath the soft warmth of
the comforter, breathing deeply, trying to calm her rattled
nerves. It bothered her that she could be a world away
from that feeling, yet it still took hold of her and reinforced
age-old insecurities in her. No matter how strong a woman
she'd become, she was still vulnerable to the vagaries of
those childhood fears. But dammit, she would not let them
win. She'd keep those curtains pulled open all night come
hell or high water.

Taylor woke with a scream, her heart racing in her
chest, her breath coming fast as she practically
hyperventilated from fear. It took her a moment to realize
where she was and that she was perfectly safe. And then

she remembered the dream that caused her to wake so suddenly and with such fright. It was one that had recurred for much of her life, ever since she and her mother lived that vagrant's lifestyle. The car, surrounded by men, scary men in Day of the Dead face paint, the terrifying white faces with blackened, hollowed eyes and stitched lips. The men pounding on the windows, trying to open the doors while Taylor cowered in a corner and her mother screamed for help that would never come.

How many times had she had this terrible nightmare? How many times had she woken her mother, only to be alone in the dark, technically still safe, but knowing that bad was all around them and the sense of safety was one that would escape her even to this day.

She needed to defy it, to not give it room to breathe, so instead of hiding beneath the blanket, as was her usual response, she forced herself out of bed, approaching the window with a sense of trepidation but a need to stop the unfounded fear from owning her as it had for far too long. She gazed up at the sky and practiced the breathing techniques she'd learned over the years to take control of her feelings. They were only thoughts, they weren't real, she told herself.

Just then the door slammed open and Sandro came running into the room wearing nothing but a pair of barely there, light green micromodal briefs.

"Are you all right?" he said, rushing toward her.

Taylor screamed again, startled as she was by the loud noise first and the mostly naked man appearing before her second. He was like the ghost of hot encounters past. *If only it was future.* Though not with him, because, well, she already knew what a charmer he was.

"What are you doing here?"

"You screamed," he said. "I had to be sure nothing was wrong."

She stopped and looked at him. "You came in here to rescue me?"

He knit his brows. "Of course I did. Well, maybe not 'rescue' you per se, but to be sure you were safe. It's not often I have houseguests screaming in the middle of the night."

Taylor blushed. How embarrassing. This was her dirty secret, her deep-seated fears. No one, but no one, knew she wrestled with this problem so regularly. And yet here was Sandro, someone she'd known only for an hour or so, rushing in to help her—in his underwear, no less.

Make that in his amazingly sexy low-cut briefs that hugged his body in a way that left nothing to the imagination. Her vivid imagination had already gotten the better of her tonight in a fearful way. But now it was starting to morph into something a bit more sexual. Because damn, he looked hot. The hard planes of his smooth chest and abs were just screaming for her to lay her hands on them. In her defense, it had been a long time since she'd romped in that playground; she'd forgotten how much fun it could be. Just looking at him made her want to dive right into that water all over again, although darn it, Sandro would hardly be one she'd want to ever have sex with. He was so grouchy he'd probably reject her anyway. Not that she'd ever proposition him.

Her eyes scanned him from his sleepy brown eyes to that sexy goatee and that long hair that her fingers wanted to weave their way through and down along that body. God, that body. Strong, corded shoulders and arms, the aforementioned chest and stomach, that tempting happy trail of hair that ended at the low-slung waistband of those itty-bitty briefs that revealed plenty of hard contours of what lay beneath the thin green fabric. Curse that waistband, the killjoy. Taylor found herself breathing hard, but this time not because she was worried about her safety but rather deeply concerned about her potential lack of control.

"Thank you, Sandro, for your concern," she said. "But I'm perfectly fine. It was all a mistake. Good night."

She reached to turn him around by his shoulders to usher him out the door, but instead she froze at the feeling of flesh on flesh. *Breathe*, she told herself.

"I'm not going anywhere until you tell me what's going on," he said, planting his feet so that she couldn't budge him.

Well, crap, Taylor thought. It was not going to be so easy to get this man out of her room before her animal impulses made her do something deeply regrettable.

Chapter Seven

SANDRO never understood the term "wifebeaters," at least when it came to when women wore the sleeveless shirts. Because looking at Taylor McFarland, her ample breasts outlined in that see-through white tee, the furthest thing from his mind was wife-beating. More like wife-worshipping. Only not wife. Make that woman-worshipping. Or if he were to be totally honest, breast-worshipping. Because at this very moment in time, even knowing Taylor was someone he needed to avoid like some sort of communicable disease he'd be stuck with for life if he wasn't careful, he wanted nothing more than to worship that body and those magnificent tits, highlighted in that beautiful, perfect, life-altering, formfitting wifebeater. It didn't help matters that the air-conditioning had left her nipples standing at attention, and he was rendered momentarily speechless as he tried to make sense of what stood before him—and what was the most forbidden of fruit, to boot.

He dragged his eyes away from her breasts long enough to notice a luscious stretch of exposed skin beneath the hem of her shirt. His eyes moved south to take in the view, which was then rudely and abruptly cut off by the strip of elastic that held in place a pair of low-cut white bikini briefs, and he thought he might pass out. Thank goodness his hands had worked their magic a few hours ago or he'd be screwed. At least figuratively, although preferably literally, as long as he was doing the screwing at least. Though he knew that was a big fat no-no. Who was he kidding? He was still screwed.

"You came to rescue me?" she said.

How to answer that question? "Well, sure, originally," he could say while hauling her by the soft tendrils of her hair into a nearby cave. "But then when I saw you looking like this, I mean, are you kidding me? Now I'm only here to fuck some sense into you, woman."

Somehow he suspected that would not be the ideal response.

His mind was still bleary with sleep, but his body had by now awoken quite readily and was quickly working its way toward full attention. Thank God the room was still dark, so maybe she wouldn't notice what he knew would soon become painfully obvious. But how could he not get a rock-hard erection with this superhot—as in *molto caldissimo* hot—woman in front of him wearing next to nothing?

Of course she would shut him down when he insisted she tell him what was wrong. Clearly whatever prompted that outburst had subsided, or she wouldn't be standing in front of the window silhouetted by the barest of moonlight, acting as if nothing had happened. But he was nothing if not stubborn, even when she pressed her hands to his shoulders, trying to force him to leave the room. But he had to know what had happened. And he had to have another chance to feel her skin on his.

"So?" he said, arching an eyebrow at her, hoping like hell she wouldn't look down at him. "What gives?"

He'd turned around so that he was facing her, and as he did so, her hands slipped off his shoulders, silently sliding down his arms as he moved his body. It sent chills up his spine and arousal to his other brain, the one over

which he had little to no control.

She glanced down at the floor, obviously not wanting to say anything more.

"Really, can't you just let it be?" she said as she began to pace in front of him.

"You screamed loud enough to rouse me from a deep sleep," he said. "The least you can do is let me know what had you so terrified."

"It's nothing. Really, it's no big deal."

He lowered his chin to his chest, looking up at her as if to say he knew that wasn't true.

"It's embarrassing."

He stopped her in her tracks and reached for her chin, staring into her blue eyes. "I know we don't really know each other. And we got off to a bad start, so you've got no reason to tell me much of anything. But I want you to know your secret's safe with me."

She squinted at him as if she was trying to figure out if she could trust him. "How can I be sure of that?"

He shrugged. "I guess I could sign it in blood, but that could get messy. Would you settle for a pinky-swear?"

She laughed. "You have pinky-swears in Italy?"

"You can't imagine the depths to which Italian culture sinks," he said. "Only here we call it a *promessa*."

"*Promessa*," she said, trying out the word. "A promise. I like that. It's more poetic."

"There are plenty more Italian, uh, things I can share with you if you're interested." *Italian things?* What the hell was that all about? Although right about now there was one very specific Italian "thing" he'd like to introduce her to.

"I'm afraid to ask." She wrinkled her nose.

"I guess that came out wrong," he said. "I just mean

culturally, and the language."

"It is a very beautiful language," she said. "One of my favorites."

"You know much Italian?"

"A bit," she said. "I'd say I'm serviceable."

"And you speak other languages?"

"Un peu de français," she said. "Y un poco de español."

He arched a brow. "So you're gifted lingually?"

She laughed. "Not sure where you're going with that, but to keep it sanitized I'll say yes, I can speak enough of a few languages to get by."

"I've been told I'm gifted lingually as well."

"Oh yeah?" she said. "If by that you mean *linguistically*, then what languages do you speak?"

"Italian and English."

"In which case I wouldn't exactly accuse you of being a polyglot."

"Polyglot?"

"Someone who speaks multiple languages."

"I never said I speak a lot of languages," he said. "I merely suggested I was good with my tongue." He smiled and winked at her. "You do know I'm teasing you though."

She rolled her eyes. "For a second there I was worried you were coming on to me."

He stepped back from her for a minute and gave her a long, hard look from head to toe. "I'd have to be dead from the waist down to not at least want to do that. Which I'm afraid you can tell is not the case."

His gaze met hers as they looked down at the same time. And then she laughed. *She freaking laughed.*

"Not quite the response a man is looking for under the

circumstances."

She frowned. "I'm so sorry. I don't mean to be rude. Though I know enough about men to know that I could be standing here in a down parka and ski pants and still you'd look like that."

He nodded his head. "I'm not going to argue with you there. But then you do this," he said, sweeping his hand from her head to her feet, "and how else could I react? A beautiful woman in a skimpy shirt and panties... Well, I'd have to be less than a man to not react this way." He tried to remember the last time he had a sort of metaphysical discussion about his hard-on with a woman he wasn't about to use it on. He couldn't come up with a single example.

"I'll bear some of the responsibility," she said, "considering you'd not be standing here were it not for my middle-of-the-night outburst."

"About that explanation..."

"Must I?" She frowned.

He motioned to the nearby love seat. "I'm all ears."

"By the way," she said, her eyebrow cocked out of curiosity. "Mint?"

"Mint?"

"Those," she said, nodding her head toward his crotch. "Did you go for mint green because it was a subliminal favorite flavor? I mean, who doesn't love mint?"

"Yes, that's why I purchased the mint-green underwear," he said. "So that women would look at me and think of dessert."

"Stranger things have happened."

"I like that you looked at me and thought about something delicious however." He gave her a wink.

"Don't flatter yourself."

"I know you're just trying to distract me from your story. The longer we discuss me, the longer you can avoid you. Unless," he said, drumming his fingers, "you'd like us to discuss your underwear."

She shook her head vigorously and raised her hands in surrender. "I give up. I'll spill it."

"I knew I'd get you to capitulate."

She put her fingers to her mouth. "Now be quiet and let me tell you about it."

Chapter Eight

"I guess I should start from the beginning."

"Begin the beguine, as it were."

She smiled dreamily. "I love that song. So romantic, from a bygone era."

"Fred Astaire, Broadway Melody of 1940."

Her eyes opened wide. "You know that film?"

He nodded. "My mother was a big fan of anything and everything to do with Fred Astaire. She wanted my father to be as light on his feet as he was. My father was a pretty good dancer, but let's just say he wasn't Fred Astaire."

They both laughed.

"My mother loved old movies as well," she said. "That is, when we were somewhere with a television where she could watch them."

"But you're American," he said. "Surely you grew up with a television in every room of your house."

She shook her head. "I know that's the impression everyone has of us, but it's not the way it is for many people in our country."

"Impossible."

"Not at all," she said. "My mother raised me on her own. My father left before I was born, and I never knew him. And Mom was left trying to sustain us both with no education and no steady income."

He leaned forward, intent. "I'm so sorry."

She pursed her lips. "I wish I could say it wasn't a big deal, but it was. Life was a struggle more often than not.

There were times when we didn't even have a roof over our heads."

His eyes widened. "In America?"

She nodded. "Of course. I know everyone thinks it is purely the land of opportunity, but for some it's not always that. Unfortunately that was the case when I was a child. My mother often worked several jobs trying to bring in enough money. But she didn't even have a high school diploma, let alone a college degree. She could only get menial jobs that paid very little. She could barely keep up the payments on our old clunker of a car. And finally we ended up out on the streets, with no place to turn, so we had to live in the car."

"You lived in a car? On the streets? How old were you?"

"Oh, on and off from when I was about five until I was about nine," she said. "Sometimes we would be able to move into a shelter, but those were dangerous. Other times she was able to scrape enough money together to find a cheap apartment. But the most steady place of residence I had was in the backseat of my mother's car."

"Were you scared?"

"Uh, yeah," she said. "You can't just park a car any old place and sleep. My mother had to find places where you could hide in the shadows. But lurking in the shadows were usually bad people as well. I was terrified."

"Did anyone ever break into the car?"

"Not when we were sleeping, thank goodness," she said. "But there were nights when I tried to sleep and we could hear men yelling nearby and swearing and shooting off guns. It was a scary place to be for a little girl."

He moved closer to Taylor and reached out to hug

Red-Hot Romeo

her. "I'm so sorry you had to live like that. It makes me feel all the worse for having so much while others have so little."

She shrugged. "It's the way of the world. Some have plenty, some don't. It's too bad that there is that imbalance, but one thing I resolved when I became famous was that I would work hard to ensure that others who were in my position have an opportunity to get past it."

"So what does this have to do with your screaming out in your sleep?"

"Oh… that," she said with a deep sigh. "It's a recurring nightmare for me. One I've had practically my whole life. It's why I always close my curtains at night: I never had a way to shut out the scary world when I was asleep in a car. And so now I try to protect myself from that when I can.

"Last night I challenged myself to keep the curtains open. You mentioned about the beautiful sunrise, and I didn't want to be that person who was so afraid of the dark that she'd miss a once-in-a-lifetime sunrise in a beautiful part of the world. I was happy with myself that I was able to drift off to sleep fine, but as happens far too often, I had the nightmare again."

"The nightmare?"

She nodded. "It begins the same every time. I'm trying to fall asleep. I'm scared because everyone can see in and I feel so vulnerable drifting off to sleep when they can see me. And I start to nod off, and then scary men gather around the car, all in that frightening face paint from the Mexican Day of the Dead: these cadaverous faces. It's so terrifying, and they're closing in on me. Honestly, I had no idea that I screamed in my sleep until you came running. I thought I just always woke up scared."

Sandro pulled her toward him, holding her tight to his chest. *"Cara mia.* It's okay. You're safe here." He rubbed her back as he cooed gentle words in Italian to soothe her. Taylor's tension loosened till she was a limp noodle while he comforted her. And as she settled into his arms, she felt the warmth of his skin against hers, and his heart pressed to hers, beating a soft tattoo next to her own. He smelled amazing. He must have taken a shower before bed because he smelled of sandalwood and earthy, masculine scents that made her feel safe and warm.

As he softly pressed his hand to the back of her head, she turned hers, and before she knew it, she found herself face-to-face with him as his eyes fixed on hers.

"Cara mia," he said, his lips gently pressed against hers. "I'm so sorry."

It wasn't her intention to follow his lead, but for some reason it was impossible not to as she opened her mouth to his, their tongues entwining while he continued to stroke her back and her hair. It was all so soothing. And erotic. And unexpected. Next thing she knew, he was easing her down against the love seat, pressing himself to her, his hands now skirting along her sides, pushing her top up a little more with each pass.

Chapter Nine

HOW did I go from wanting to slap this man to getting downright horizontal with him in about ten seconds flat?

There were unanswered mysteries in the world, and for now this appeared to be one of them. But… while it might not be a solvable one, it would have to be a resolvable one because she could not do this. Not with this man. Not right now. Not here.

She'd seen what he was like a few short hours ago. He was not a man she wanted to get down and dirty with. Probably not even down and clean with. He had issues with women; she could tell that just by his reaction to Luca's announcement. And she just really wasn't in a place in her life where she wanted to deal with that sort of thing. Besides, she was here to have a nice, relaxing weekend and attend the big launch of the winery, not get to third and a half base—because it seemed they were fast approaching there unless the pitcher could strike him out—somewhere between going to sleep for the night and the dawn's crowing of roosters, which she was pretty sure she was hearing faintly beyond the sound of their heavy breathing.

Must. Put. Stop. To. This. Now.

But shoot. She was kind of having fun. And, well, wow. He was a really good kisser. Which she was surprised she'd even participated in with morning breath and all—or middle-of-the-night breath at least. Maybe that mint underwear of his somehow enhanced the breath at four in the morning or whatever time it was. For that matter, she'd barely slept; she was tired! She needed to get to bed in order to get up and not miss breakfast. Which all sounded like ridiculous excuse-making when in fact she just knew she needed to put a halt to this before she became inextricably tangled up with a man who had woman problems. So not on her agenda.

She had already washed her hands of the love-'em-and-leave-'em type she'd grown weary of. The men who thought it was some sort of trophy they needed to win, to get in the pants of a famous supermodel. No, thank you. First of all, she might be a model, but she knew she wasn't any more super than anyone else. She just happened to have good genes and knew how to play the game well so that she landed modeling jobs. Nothing about that should be part of the decision-making when anyone was planning to hook up with her. Even though by hooking up she didn't mean that sort of hooking up but rather getting together in a more clothes-off manner. Because really, she was not a fan of the one-nighter anyhow. Not her scene.

All this mental rambling meant Sandro had that much more time to get his hands up her wifebeater tank and *oh God, that felt so good,* she thought as he toyed with her nipple at the same time he nuzzled her ear: her Kryptonite combo. Meanwhile, his other hand had mysteriously slipped around her, and his fingers quickly slid beneath her bikini panties and wow, his warm hands on her behind were really quite nice.

Taylor wrestled back and forth in her head with how to end this and when to end it and whether or not to end it, but she knew she had to even as his tongue trailed down her neck, and then before she knew what was happening, his mouth settled over that nipple and *oh God, please don't stop please don't stop please don't stop.* But she had to put an end to this madness. Even while that other sneaky hand was insinuating its way below the waistband of the front of her panties and *oh, right there, oh yes.*

Oh no.

Oh maybe?

His fingers slid into that very spot, and she let out a moan and he let out a groan and he bit down on her nipple. *He bit her!* But it felt so good, how could she make him stop when it was exactly what the doctor ordered? Not that there was a doctor ordering this for her, but if there were, this was precisely what his prescription would call for: Sandro's fingers moving through her slick center, circling feverishly around that swollen flesh, just where no man had been in about a thousand years, give or take a millennia. And the more he worked his magical fingers on her, and the more his mouth nipped and licked and sucked on her breast, the more she became mute, incapable of speaking and instead only feeling, and if she was to be honest, she was feeling pretty darned good, thanks.

She pressed her pelvis toward his enthusiastic fingers, encouraging him to slide a couple inside her while his thumb continued to play her like an instrument. Her breathing became fraught as she thrust toward his hands even more insistently until finally she went over the top, electricity ripping through her body, her synapses on overload as she shouted his name so loudly it crashed through her sensual trance long enough to break the spell altogether.

She pushed her hands against Sandro's shoulders, and even as he resisted she insisted.

"*Cara,*" he said. "What is it?"

"I'm sorry, Sandro. I'm afraid I got carried away. This should not have happened."

"But *carissima*. You don't really mean that. We've been having so much fun. Why would you want to end things now?"

Taylor sat up, shifting her T-shirt back down and pulling her panties back up and acting as if she'd just gotten busted by her parents after a steamy make-out session with her sixteen-year-old boyfriend in the family room. Not that she'd ever had that experience since she'd never brought boys home to the temporary places she'd inhabited as a kid. Boy, did she screw this one up. She couldn't even tell Larkin about this because she'd never hear the end of it.

But one thing was for sure: what happened right now was the end of that. It was unfortunate that he was likely going to look at her like she was a total cock tease, which she wasn't. At least not under normal circumstances. It's just that she'd let things get away from her. It was the strangest of circumstances, the intimacy of a dark night, the connection over a scary experience, the security of strong arms and a warm body. Totally understandable. It would happen to most people, she was sure of that. But for now it was time to usher him out of her room.

Poor Sandro trudged uncomfortably out of the room with that hard-on of his getting in his way; his mint-green bikini briefs had seemingly taken on a life of their own. And while part of her wanted nothing more than to reach down to that tasty-looking mint package he'd gladly offered her for dessert, the other part of her knew she was wise and responsible to nip this in the bud.

She closed the door behind a fuming Sandro and pressed her body against it, just in case he tried to open it

and insinuate his way back in.

It was then that she looked toward the wall of windows to see the most extraordinary sunrise: sleepy fingers of mauve and melon and rose creeping over the horizon and then the smallest semicircle of orange-ish-peach peeking along the edge of the distant mountains. It was breathtaking.

And she couldn't help but think she wished she'd let Sandro stick around to enjoy it with her. Instead, the only cock she was left with was the one crowing not far outside her bedroom window.

Chapter Ten

IT was a fucking glorious orange sunrise, yet all he had to show for it was a set of painful blue balls. Seemed like the only cock that got much of a workout in the past two hours was that damned rooster crowing his pleasure to the outside world. Of course the ice princess got what she needed but then promptly shut the gates to the castle tight.

Tight. Crap. The word made him think of where his fingers had been only a few minutes earlier: tight and wet and practically calling his name until she went all icebox on him. What the hell made women do that? Is it that they had some sort of sexual buyer's remorse just before they hit the jackpot? Well, before the guy hit the jackpot at any rate. He'd rung her bell, and she'd seemed to be quite satisfied not only with the results but the process as well.

And now Sandro lay in bed, his hand on his cock, trying to put an end to the poor thing's suffering so perhaps he could have a few hours of sleep. The last thing he needed was to be exhausted. He'd been willing to make that sacrifice if it had ultimately been worth it, but instead, what did he get? A good time, punctuated by mixed messages, finalized by a veritable guillotine drop. At least he was able to spare having the thing lopped off. He'd have to be grateful for that, for lack of anything better.

Sandro had a black cloud looming over his head as he worked his way toward the terrace for breakfast. So what that the weather was beautiful, the sun shining, the birds chirping? He was still fuming over the Frigidaire maneuver by that damned model, and he was in a sour mood.

As he walked out onto the terrace, which boasted a spectacular view of vineyards and olive groves in the Chianti hillside, he saw Luca and Larkin seated at the table, enjoying their morning cappuccinos. *Damned happy lovebirds.*

"*Buon giorno*, Alessandro," Luca said in his best Italian. But the last thing Sandro wanted was for anyone to try to persuade him it was a good morning, because it was decidedly no such thing. So he merely gave a nod and sat down to wait for the maid to serve him his breakfast.

Luca and Larkin looked at each other.

"Well," Luca said. "Looks like someone woke up on the wrong side of the bed."

"Shame," Larkin said, "Because our bed was so comfy." She winked at her fiancé.

Which was precisely the worst thing she could have said.

"Look." Sandro's brows knit in annoyance. "If the two of you are happily going at it all night long, well good for you. But you don't need to rub it in."

"Oh ho ho," Luca said. "I guess I was right last night: you do need to get laid."

If only he knew the half of it.

"I need nothing of the sort. I simply don't want the likes of you two rubbing it in."

"Better than you rubbing one out, you mean?" Luca said, chucking his cousin on the shoulder.

Just then Sandro heard heels on the stone terrace and looked up to see Taylor breezing in wearing a short, flowy light blue sundress that made her look downright angelic, dammit.

He took one look at her and quickly glanced away. He was going to pretend absolutely nothing had happened. Because, well, nothing was going to happen, so what sense was there in beating that dead horse? He'd only get grief from Luca, and if Luca mentioned it to Larkin, well, of course it would get right back to the ice princess, and that would only further humiliate him. And hell hath no fury like a scorned man with blue balls. Or something like that.

"Morning, everybody," she said with a smile as Luca stood to pull out her chair for her to sit down. Right next to Sandro, because, well, why not?

She nodded to him. "Sandro. I trust you slept well."

Ooooh, some nerve for her to dare suggest that in front of all of them.

He nodded back. "Ahhh... *La principessa di ghiaccio.*" He turned back to his phone where he remained glued while Luca and Larkin looked at each other, confusion on their faces at him calling her the ice princess.

"Everything okay, my friend?" Luca said.

"Magnificent," he said, his arms wide and pointed to the sky. "Couldn't be better. I mean after all, look at this

day. I'm about to share my dream come true with the world. What could be wrong?"

He took a sip of his espresso, setting the cup down a little bit hard, nearly breaking the thing.

The maid came out and brought Taylor a *spremuta*— fresh-squeezed orange juice—along with her cappuccino.

"You sleep well, Tay?" Luca asked.

"My room was lovely, and the bed was divine," she said. "I was up for a while in the middle of the night, but that's to be expected."

Sandro about spit his espresso all over the table on that one.

"Huh. I didn't think you'd have a problem with jet lag since you'd just come from London," Larkin said. "Only an hour's difference."

Taylor sighed. "I guess sometimes that's all it takes to wake with a start in the middle of the night."

"My apologies," Sandro said through gritted teeth. "I had hoped to make your stay as comfortable as possible. Perhaps I didn't do enough in that regard?"

He looked up at Taylor, who stared deep into her cappuccino as if there were some hidden message at the bottom of her cup. Again, Luca and Larkin glanced at each other, their brows knit.

"Uh, is there something we're missing out on?" Luca said, taking a bite of his *cornetto* pastry.

"What are you talking about?" Sandro said, shredding into his own *cornetto alla marmellata* as if it were his life's mission. And of course a blob of jam fell from it onto his shirt. As much as he didn't want to discuss the matter, the more he thought about it, the more he wanted to see Taylor squirm a bit. "I was sound asleep. You'll have to ask

Taylor, because evidently she's the one with sleep issues."

Taylor threw him enough shade to block out the morning sun.

She shook her head. "I don't know why everyone's making a big deal of this. I slept *fine*."

"See, Luca," Larkin said. "She's fine." She looked over at her friend as if to ask if that was true, but Taylor continued to not make eye contact with anyone.

"So what's on the agenda today?" Luca said, turning to Sandro. "Anything we can do to help in preparation for tomorrow night?"

He shook his head. "I think it's all on me now. My brothers will be helping with the final touches as well, but I'm in charge, so I've got to take care of the details."

"In that case, if you're good with us enjoying the pool, I think it's calling our name," Luca said, looking down to the infinity pool below.

"By all means," Sandro said with a sweep of his hands. "What's mine is yours." He looked long and hard at Taylor, trying to send a message to her, but she only averted her gaze. Of course, he wasn't sure what that message was because if last night taught him anything, it was not to get involved with women with issues. Make that women, period. And certainly women who would probably cut off your left nut if given the chance. He wanted to keep those where they were, thanks, and also couldn't afford to be left standing high and dry like that again, so he'd just avoid Taylor McFarland altogether.

Chapter Eleven

THE temperature was perfect—unusually comfortable for late June in Tuscany. Taylor, Larkin, and Luca lounged by the pool, the two women chatting and gossiping while Luca sifted through paperwork for upcoming appearances he had for the royal family.

The infinity pool appeared to crest over the edge to the countryside below. The view was breathtaking: fields and fields of ripening grapes and groves of ancient, gnarled olive trees. The sky was one of those pristine bluebird blues, the type so invitingly pure you just want to stare at it endlessly.

The pool was surrounded by butterfly bushes and beds of purple, pink, and yellow flowers. Butterflies and bees flitted in and out amidst the lavender and rosemary that grew along one wall.

"You mind handing me that sunscreen, Tay?" Larkin said. "By the way, it looks like you're starting to burn. You might want to put some more on yourself."

"Thanks for the heads-up," she said. "I'll take care of that after you and Luca take a turn with it."

"I appreciate it, Taylor, but I'm good," Luca said. "I've got that Mediterranean blood, so I don't burn so easily. Must be the Italian in me from my father's side."

"It's what makes them so darned sexy," Larkin said as she leaned over to kiss Luca. "Those blue eyes and white teeth set against that deep, beautiful tan... Irresistible."

Taylor laughed because at first Luca had been anything

but irresistible to Larkin. The woman had avoided him like the plague when she first met him while covering Milan's Fashion Week.

"Funny how you've changed your tune about him," she whispered to her friend.

"Speaking of changing tunes," Larkin said. "That was really strange at breakfast between you and Sandro. Did something happen last night after we went to our room?" She opened the bottle of sunscreen and squeezed a thin band of it along her leg and proceeded to massage it in.

Taylor feigned ignorance. "Gosh, Lark, I just went to bed. I don't know what you think would have happened."

"It's just that the two of you seemed to have some weird undercurrent of unspoken words going on there this morning," she said. "I mean on the one hand Luca and I would have loved for you and Sandro to hit it off, but last night it sure seemed like the two of you weren't exactly destined for a date, let alone a future together.

"So sure, of course you two would be weird together this morning. After all, that's how it was before we went to bed. I guess I'd hoped that maybe it was just late, everyone was tired, and things would be better in the morning."

Taylor was thrilled that her friend had talked herself out of the very argument she was uncertain how to defend against. The last thing she wanted was to get those two involved in her stupid mistake. Best that no one know about what had gone on between her and Sandro, which would keep things from becoming even more awkward anyhow.

Sandro had been back and forth across huge swaths of the property what seemed like several times over the course of the past few hours. At first he'd wanted to walk, despite the distances, just to help get his head on straight. He could always clear his mind with some vigorous exercise, and he really needed to empty his brain of any of that nonsense from last night. But now he was tired and hungry and regretting he hadn't taken the Piaggio Ape, a small utility vehicle with three wheels often found throughout Italy. Sort of like a Vespa with a flatbed on the back. It was the easiest way to maneuver along steep and narrow paths in the vineyards and often the simplest thing with which to haul supplies. Right now he wished he had an Ape nearby so he could attempt to curl up in the flatbed and take a nap.

If he couldn't satisfy his fatigue, at least he could slake his need to cool down with a quick dip in the pool. He stripped off his shirt while he crested the hillside. As he turned the corner approaching the pool though, he stopped dead in his tracks when he saw Taylor applying sunscreen to that pretty-darned-perfect body of hers. It was the damnedest thing that a person slathering on sunscreen could be arousing, but she was. At least right here, right now, as she stroked her hands up her endlessly long legs, then massaged lotion onto her flat stomach, next slipping her fingers beneath her skimpy top to make sure she didn't burn along the edges of her very tiny hot-pink bikini.

Mamma mia, that woman was going to be the death of him.

Sandro had just decided to wait till the now semipermanent bulge in his pants calmed down before making an appearance at the pool when Luca spotted him.

"Sandro," Luca said, waving him over. "*Andiamo*. Let's go! We were just about to take a dip."

"You go ahead without me," Sandro said. "I'll be there in a minute. I have to get my suit on."

"Don't worry about formalities," Luca said. "We're all friends here. I'm sure whatever you've got on under your jeans is pretty much what your suit would be like anyhow. Just take your pants off and get over here."

Sandro shrugged his shoulders, resigned to the inevitable. "Fine. Give me a minute."

Larkin and Luca both got up and walked to the edge of the pool, but Taylor remained on the chaise longue. She was taking a swig of her water, and Sandro wanted nothing more than to grab that body and slowly drip the water along her glistening flesh. And then maybe lick it off. Except that he didn't want to do that! Hell no! He was steering so clear of that woman he would practically be on the other side of the country from her. Except that now he had to get in the pool. With any luck she'd stay seated, so at least he'd not have her too close to him, taunting him with her mere presence.

With the bulge finally settled down enough, Sandro maneuvered around the landscaping and entered the pool along a stone path. He approached a chair on the other side of the pool from Taylor, as far away as could be, untied his

boots and toed them off, removed his socks, then pulled down his jeans. His briefs today were sky blue, but that was about the only difference in them. In fact, what both he and Taylor had on too closely replicated their sleepwear from the night before, only Taylor's was even more revealing. He vowed to not look, just to be sure temptation didn't get the best of him.

"Come in," Larkin said. "The water feels great!" She splashed Sandro enough for him to realize that his briefs became a bit see-through when wet. *Well, good,* he thought. *Give her a little taste of what she missed out on.* With renewed confidence, Sandro strolled to the side of the pool, stretched his arms, loosened up his tight lower back, and then dove in, creating quite a splash.

"Thanks for that," Taylor said with a frown as she held up her magazine, dripping water from Sandro's wall of water.

"Put it down, it'll dry out," Larkin said. "And get your butt in here!"

Sandro wondered if she was doing the same thing as him, keeping her distance, playing it safe. But finally after enough haranguing from the other two, Taylor got up, secured the two thin straps of her bikini behind her neck, then threw her head back to straighten out her hair, or whatever it was women did that for. Dramatic effect? Who the hell knew. But it looked hot, which was unfortunate, because that nagging little appendage of his instantly responded. Which got even worse when she stood on the edge of the pool, her long, lithe body on display, her breasts just barely covered by two meager patches and her bikini bottoms a mere thong, leaving little to his vivid and undersatisfied imagination.

He wondered for a minute what it would be like to just grab her, pull her into the water, and wrap her legs around his waist. Would that be such a bad thing?

Hell yes, it would be a terrible thing. So terrible. But even more terrible was that just as Taylor was about to dive in, those skimpy strings that held her top up slipped loose, and for a fleeting handful of seconds, Sandro got his fill of two of the most beautiful breasts he'd seen in ages. And he could tell by the near evenness of the skin tone across her chest that "bathing suit top optional" was likely her preferred means of sunbathing. And only here did she deem it important to cover herself up.

God, he was doomed.

Chapter Twelve

THE two of them could not have kept a farther distance from each other in the pool. It was like a seventh grade dance with the boys on one side, the girls on the other. Complete with Luca and Larkin pawing at each other in the middle, just like you'd have had with the golden couple in the darkest corner of the school gymnasium. And of course there was Taylor, having just flashed her boobs in front of the opposition's eyeballs, wanting to shrink into the background, only there was no place to shrivel away to. Ugh.

This weekend was clearly going to test her stamina in resisting that man, and it sure didn't help that he looked so damned hot in his briefs yet again. So hot it made her wonder what was wrong with her for having pulled the plug on things earlier this morning. Because right now, *ay, ay, ay,* she was having a hard time keeping her eyes off his gorgeous body. She simply had to resolve to just move on, pretend whatever had gone on hadn't really happened. How else would she get through swimming half-naked with the man in the same body of water?

"So," she said, struggling a bit for a topic. "How was your morning?"

He looked at her and frowned. "Before, during, or after?"

She about choked on that one, never expecting him to vocalize anything to do with what had gone down. Oh God. Thank goodness *that* hadn't happened at least. Even though if she were a betting woman, she'd wager he'd be reallllly good at that based on what a skillful kisser he was.

She dipped her chin and threw him a glare. "How about while preparing for the grand opening?"

"Which one?"

She wanted to throttle him. Perhaps an accidental drowning would be a possibility? Luca and Larkin wouldn't even notice, the way they were so engrossed in one another.

"You've got more than one grand opening going on at a time, dude?" Luca—who clearly had mastered his own art of multitasking—piped in.

Sandro sighed. "Let's just say I had another sort of, uh, soft project I was trying, *hard*, to get into. The grand opening would have been spectacular, as it was really *slick*," he said, glancing at Taylor. "Unfortunately, the whole thing got shut down prematurely."

Taylor wanted to scream. The insolence of the man!

"I didn't know you had anything else big going on," Luca said.

"Oh, this would have been *big*," Sandro said. "Big. Oh." He looked at her and smiled broadly.

You bastard, she mouthed at him. The last thing she wanted was for Luca to know about what had happened. A maid entered the pool area and delivered glasses of white wine to each of them. Taylor took a sip, closing her mind to what was happening and instead savoring the refreshing, citrusy tang of her wine.

"That's a shame," Luca said. "I'd love to hear more about it. I wonder if there's a backdoor way to get back in with it?"

Sandro shook his head, a look of disappointment on

his face. "I'm afraid not. The principle was pretty adamant that while my skills were most desirable and I could prove my high degree of success, there was no way for any sharing to occur. Think of it like a one-night stand: come and gone." He snapped his fingers for emphasis.

Taylor spat out her mouthful of wine before she could swallow.

"Everything okay, Taylor?" Sandro asked. "Anything I can do to, uh, please you?"

Larkin looked at Sandro with confusion in her face. "That's sort of a weird thing to say when someone chokes. Tay—you all right?"

Taylor fanned her face as if to wave away the uncomfortable choking sensation. "Sorry. Must've gone down the wrong pipe."

"Speaking of going down," Sandro said.

Oh my God, I am so going to kill him when I get him alone. Even though I can't ever be alone with him since I don't trust myself—or him—for one measly minute.

"Look at those beautiful butterflies," Taylor said, aiming for a diversionary change of subject. "I've never seen anything so gorgeous. They're sort of striped with that royal blue. Spectacular. Don't you just love nature?"

Sandro sipped his wine, watching her over his glass. "Nature is at its finest when left to unfold as nature would want. Don't you agree, Taylor?"

"Have you been drinking?" Larkin said to him. "It's like you're speaking in some weird code."

"Right?" Taylor said. "Maybe you should go lie down and clear your head. The stress of the day must be getting to you."

"To the contrary," he said. "I suspect it's the lying

down that got to me. I think I'd rather keep it *up*."

"Gosh, I'm starving," Taylor said, looking at her watch for emphasis. "Anybody else ready for lunch?"

She waded to the stone steps in the shallow end of the pool and stepped out. After toweling off, she wrapped a sarong around her tanned waist and threw a pleading look to Larkin to come to her rescue.

"Oh, and a word of advice, ice princess," Sandro said in a whisper as he toweled off his hair. "Keep the top off. No need messing up your tan on my account." With a wink, he strode away from her, leaving her to just want to throttle him all the more.

Chapter Thirteen

ALESSANDRO was confident he'd gotten his point across to Taylor. Although to put a finer point on it, he wasn't quite clear himself on what that point even was. Was he trying to let her know that the "help wanted" sign was still posted in his window, just in case she changed her mind? Or did he just want to feed her a fat slice of guilt pie because she'd done him wrong? If not wrong, then at least not right.

Of course, she was perfectly entitled to shut him down like she did and was under no obligation whatsoever to have continued with their little—what would you call it? Dalliance? Demi-tryst? Fooling around? A massive tease? But still, it was, at the very least, disappointing. Good thing he had bigger things on his mind to worry about. Except that for some reason, this was overriding those vastly more relevant issues. He needed to get back to work and stop this nonsense.

Everyone else had gotten out of the pool and was drying off.

"I'll leave you all to enjoy *pranzo*," he said. "No relaxing lunch for me today. Too much to do."

"Sandro, you need to eat," Larkin said, locking arms with him. "I think all the stress of getting ready for the launch has gone to your head. Come relax and enjoy some downtime. Besides, what would we talk about if you weren't there?"

He could only imagine what might be discussed,

though he certainly was under the impression that Taylor was keeping their secret to herself. Nevertheless, his curiosity got the better of him.

"Fine, but only for a short while," he said. "Let me just check in with my brother to be sure everything is under control. I'll meet you on the terrace."

He made a quick call to Matteo, who reassured him he wasn't needed. By the time he arrived at the table, they were eating antipasti.

"This is fantastic prosciutto," Taylor said with a moan. Did she really have to do that? Last time he'd heard that sound of satisfaction emanating from her throat, it was under far more promising circumstances.

"*Cinta Senese*," he said. "A special breed of pig a good friend of mine in Siena raises. It's like no other."

"It melts in your mouth," Larkin said as she shared a piece with Luca. "Here, taste, baby." And he literally ate it from her mouth, like the mongrels in *Lady and the Tramp* with the spaghetti. Somehow slightly less romantic with thinly sliced meat however.

That said, to be at a table with people eating practically from each other's mouths suggested an intimacy that those outside that circle of familiarity just might covet. For instance, on some level Sandro wouldn't have minded being close enough to a woman that he'd want to do that with her. However, he could never imagine him so doing: he'd just never been with any woman who instilled that sort of carnal need in him. Thank God. Because who had time for that level of dedication? It would certainly put a crimp in your independence, no doubt about that.

He looked over and noticed Taylor watching them with a wistful knit in her brow.

"You two are so darned sweet together," she said, resting her chin on the palms of her hands as she gazed at her friends. She looked all swoony, like a teenager at the malt shop, in love with being in love. "I'm so glad you found each other."

Dagger to the heart. Because Sandro had mixed feelings about them finding each other. Sure, he was perfectly glad that his friend was so happy. But of course he was not so thrilled that he got stuck on the outside looking in, his nose pressed to the steamy window while those inside feasted on a Christmas goose.

"Yep," he said with a grimace. "Downright adorable."

Taylor glared at him. "You're just jealous."

"At least I make an effort."

Taylor curled her lip in a snarl.

Luca cocked an eyebrow at his friend. "What is up with you, man? I don't think I've ever seen you so tense before. Maybe you need to schedule a massage."

Sandro refilled everyone's wineglasses. "I just need to get through tomorrow, and I'll be fine."

"If you're sure," Larkin said with a concerned frown. "We're just worried about you."

"I'm so tired of talking about me," he said. "Let's discuss something else."

"Fine idea. Tay, what's up with your charity?" Luca asked.

Taylor blushed with the attention suddenly turned on her.

"Oh well, I've been fundraising to bring in more full-time workers in each of the countries we're in," she said. "But the amount of money we need means I've got my work cut out for me."

Sandro looked at her. "Your charity?"

"It's called Rags to Riches. We help underprivileged kids get stylish, up-to-date clothes to wear so they don't feel like outcasts all the time."

He cocked his head. "Really? How interesting."

"I think so," she said. "I mean, it's not stopping starvation or anything, but it's a largely overlooked aspect of poverty and affects poor children, like it or not. It's awful to not have a meal, but it's also humiliating to show up in donated hand-me-downs with food stains and holes in them. Think how hard it is for those kids to integrate into social circles at school. And how important that socialization is for young children."

Sandro stared at her intently, focusing for once on her words rather than her looks. Wow. Seemed Miss Taylor McFarland had a business and philanthropic head on her beautiful shoulders.

A maid brought out the *primi piatto*: *spaghetti al sugo di pomodoro e basilica*, a simple spaghetti with tomato basil sauce.

"So this charity of yours," Sandro said, nodding his thanks to the maid. "How is it that it came about?"

"Well, I already told you about my childhood," she said as he nodded. "It left its mark on me, of course. And I vowed that someday when I could, I would try to do something to mitigate the problem for others. I don't profess to have all the answers to childhood poverty, and I'm no expert on many of the needs of poor children. I just knew this was something I could do. I'm able to tap into my extensive connections in the fashion world for donations, but also I can use the access that I've been afforded in my position to raise money as well."

"Brava," Sandro said. "I'm very impressed with your work. Remind me, and I'll be sure to write you a check."

Taylor tilted her head, trying to make sense of this kinder, gentler version of Sandro. Of course, she'd seen into that window already, though not for long before it fogged up and obscured the view. But it was awfully intriguing, such moments of insight. Clearly, Sandro was a complicated man. Shame she didn't have time for such complications in her life.

Chapter Fourteen

LUCA was sound asleep on the chaise longue after lunch, and Larkin and Taylor were floating on rafts in the pool.

"Um, Tay?" Larkin said. "Exactly when did you tell Sandro about your childhood?"

Taylor froze. "What do you mean?"

"At lunch. You mentioned that you'd already told him about your childhood. That's kind of odd since we only just got here and the two of you have been sparring the whole time. Then the other thing is that I've never known you to discuss your childhood, and certainly not with a virtual stranger. I'm one of few people who knows anything about it, and I don't know much. Something is kind of fishy here."

Virtual stranger... Oh God, Taylor thought. I got hot and heavy with a man I didn't even know!

Taylor rolled off the raft and into the water. She leaned forward, her elbows on the raft, facing Larkin.

"So...," she said, biting her lip. "Forgive me, Father, for I have sinned?"

"Sinned?" her friend echoed.

"Um, did I ever mention to you about my nightmares?"

Larkin lowered her sunglasses to have a better look at Taylor's face. "Nooo..."

"I have nightmares a lot," she said. "It's always the same one."

"I'm sorry, Tay," Larkin said. "That's awful. What is it

that plagues you so badly in your sleep?"

"Well, you know I wasn't always a fabulous supermodel," she said with an exaggerated wink as she fake-primped her wet hair.

"Really?" Larkin said. "I thought you came out of the womb that way."

"*Au contraire*," she said, wagging her finger. "It was nothing of the sort."

"Well, I hate to even mention what I was like in my pathetic youth."

"I bet I could top it."

"Nerd band girl. Polyester uniform with flood pants and big black glasses. You?"

Taylor shook her head. "Sorry, can't picture you in the marching band. Please don't tell me you played the tuba."

Larkin rolled her eyes. "Hell no. Flute. I went for the delicate instrument."

"The one where you really learn to pucker."

"Please," Larkin said, pointing at her lips. "There was no puckering happening with these things for basically ever."

"You're not alone there," Taylor said. "I was almost six feet tall by the time I was in seventh grade, so you can imagine how that worked out for me."

"Yeah, all the vertically challenged boys looking skyward at you would not have been so desirable," she said. "For that matter, their faces would've been right in your boobs."

"More like just about crotch-level. You'd have thought they'd be all over me."

They laughed.

"But what does this have to do with your nightmares?"

Larkin asked.

"We were dirt poor," she said. "Had absolutely nothing. I remember eating canned beans for weeks in a row. That was it."

"Wow," Larkin said. "That's awful."

"My mother would get them at the dollar store. I think she thought the beans had some nutritional value, but honestly they could have been put to better use as mortar for bricklayers," she said. "But she already couldn't afford to put a roof over our head. So if she had to choose between shelter and food, of course food won. Even if it barely qualified as fit for human consumption."

"But you must have lived somewhere."

Taylor frowned. She really hated talking about this, and all of a sudden it seemed to be the topic *du jour*. "We lived in my mother's beat-up old car."

Larkin gasped quietly and placed her hand over her mouth. "Oh, Taylor. I'm so sorry. That's tragic."

Taylor nodded. "It wasn't exactly the best of times. But we had each other, so at least there was that."

"So this is what your nightmares are about?"

"It's that, but it's like really bad people are trying to attack us in the car," she said. "I think it's like the combination of some creepy horror film I must've seen at some point and just little flickers of memories from that time."

"Do you remember it well?"

"Yes and no," she said. "I try not to recall it really. There's nothing about that time that evokes good feelings in me. Though it's so imprinted in me it's hard to completely forget. But it's why I started my charity."

"Ah," Larkin said, understanding dawning on her face

as her eyes opened wide. "I get it now. I thought you just did that because you love clothes."

"It's because I knew how much I would have loved something like that when I was little."

"You're a good woman to do such a thing," Larkin said. "But what does this all have to do with Sandro?"

Taylor pushed her sunglasses to the top of her head and squeezed her eyes tight. "Will you think less of me if I tell you something that might make you think less of me?"

Larkin cocked an eyebrow. "Of course not, but man, you'd better tell me now or I'll kill you."

Taylor sighed. "I had that nightmare last night. Which isn't totally surprising. But what I didn't realize is apparently I scream out in my sleep! Who knew?"

"I've never heard you do that, and we've slept together plenty."

"Yeah, but I don't have the nightmare every night. Maybe it's more common when I'm in a strange place?"

"That would make sense," Larkin said. "So you screamed and then somehow I lost respect for you?"

"I was kind of shaken when I woke up," Taylor said. "I got up and was looking out the window, which is kind of weird for me because I always keep the curtains closed at night. Sort of fallout from my childhood. I like to feel secure."

"Poor girl."

Taylor shrugged. Poor girl? Not really. In the entirety of her whole life, she knew she was a pretty lucky girl. Just not so much in her sleep apparently. "As I was staring out the window at the stars in the sky, Sandro came rushing in to see what was the matter. Apparently he'd heard me scream."

"Awww," Larkin said. "That's the Sandro we know and love. He was so grumpy last night, but that's so unusual for him! Okay, we've got Sandro to the rescue. Now get to the part where I don't respect you anymore."

Taylor playfully swatted at her head. "Well first of all, he came racing into my room in like, nothing."

Larkin's eyes were wide. "As in no clothes? You mean you got to see him naked?"

"No! No! Gosh, no!"

"But you said he was in nothing."

"Okay, so it was pretty much next to nothing, but it wasn't altogether nothing," Taylor said. "Like the skimpiest little bikini briefs you can imagine. The kind that leaves pretty much nothing to your imagination."

"I'm actually surprised he doesn't sleep naked."

"Maybe he does," Taylor said. "Maybe he threw something on really quickly to be decent."

"But wouldn't you try to actually *be* decent if you were going to do that? Like if that were me, I'd put on some pants, a robe, *something*."

"I'm not sure if I need to psychoanalyze his intent when he threw on teeny tiny underwear," Taylor said. "He's a guy. I'm impressed he got that far."

"So he runs in wearing his underwear," Larkin said. "Then what?"

Taylor shook her head. "You're making this sound very titillating."

"That's because it is," she said. "Go on. You've got me on pins and needles."

"So then I mean I had to explain why I was shouting things in my sleep."

"And?"

"And he listened. And we talked."

"That's all?"

Taylor frowned. "Well…," she said and covered her eyes in embarrassment. "Not exactly."

Larkin clapped her hands with excitement, and Taylor shushed her so as not to wake up Luca. "I told Luca you two would be good together!"

Taylor's eyes got wide. "Dammit. I knew you were trying to fix us up. I told you not to do that! Well, serves you right, because no such thing will happen. Trust me on that."

Larkin snapped her fingers. "Darn."

"Believe me, it is so for the better."

"Well what's the deal? He runs in to save you, you talk, but now you're totally averse to him?"

"The feeling is mutual, I'm sure."

"Did you punch him or something?"

"Argh," Taylor said. "Do I really have to get into the details of things? Can't we just leave it at we're not going on a date anytime soon? Or ever, for that matter?"

"But why?"

"Okay, fine," she said. "I'll tell you, but you are so sworn to secrecy on this. No talking to him either." She pointed her thumb over her shoulder to a snoring Luca.

"Cross my heart," Larkin said, tracing her finger in an X across her chest.

"So we talked and talked and talked," Taylor said. "And it was strange because it felt like we'd known each other for ages. He was very sweet and listened intently as I confessed to these deep, dark fears I've never shared with anyone. Which was weird all on its own that I'd discuss them with him."

Larkin rested her elbows on her raft, her fingers linked, her chin resting on them as she sat in rapt attention.

"And then I don't know exactly what happened, but it went from talking to action. I guess he felt bad for me, and then he hugged me and, I mean we were both in our underwear, which isn't exactly conducive to chastity, amiright?"

"You had sex? On a first date? Which wasn't even a date? Although it was a very chivalrous rescue, so practically skip-to-second-date points for that."

"We didn't have sex!"

Larkin's shoulder sank. "You didn't? Rats. I was really hoping you did."

"So much for your judging me for such a thing. I think I just got knocked down a notch for cutting it off!"

"Well, why on earth did you do that anyhow?"

"It all just happened so crazy fast," Taylor said. "And I don't even know him. Even though it felt like I did. But it just seemed like that was a bad idea from the get-go. I mean seriously, can you imagine that I said good night to you two and he was so surly and then if we'd have shown up to breakfast with that glow about us? How weird would that have been?"

"Well, you practically did that," Larkin said. "Only instead, something happened. I mean now that I think about it, you looked fine. It was Sandro who was surly."

Taylor grimaced and blushed.

Larkin looked at her. "Oooooh," she said, rubbing her hands together. "Now I think I'm getting it. So you, well, you were all good to go, so to speak, but then you stopped it before it went any further. Leaving Sandro to be Master of His Domain. Dot dot dot."

"What are you talking about?"

"It's a famous *Seinfeld* episode," Larkin said. "It was referring to you know." She nudged her.

"You know?"

"Let's just say he had to play his flute solo," Larkin said. "In keeping with the marching band theme."

Taylor smacked her again jokingly. "Ewww. Leave my flute out of this thing."

"It's not your flute we're talking about, honey."

"Let's leave all flutes out of this then."

"So am I correct that basically you panicked, things felt out of control, and so you gave him the old heave-ho just as things were going his way?"

"Yes." She sighed. "That's it in a nutshell."

Larkin arched her brow.

"Would you stop inferring sexual references in my words already?" Taylor said. "As it is, I feel bad enough. But still, he got so grumpy today it reaffirmed I'd made the right decision."

"He seemed fine at lunch."

"An aberration."

"Look, Taylor," Larkin said. "I'm not going to push you into something with the man, but you could do worse. He's usually a really sweet guy, and he's available. How rare is that? And well, this place is hardly shabby, so added bonus points."

"I appreciate your kind concern, Lark," Taylor said. "But I think this weekend I'll enjoy some R & R, take advantage of the opportunity to do some fundraising Saturday night, and we'll call it a weekend. I just have no interest in your typical rich, haughty, Italian man."

"It's your weekend to call as you like, but it might be

more fun if it had a bit of a climax, if you know what I mean." She elbowed Taylor in the ribs.

"Hope you're not planning on a career in comedy anytime soon."

"That bad, huh?"

Nodding, Taylor said, "Come on. We're turning into prunes. I'm done angsting over this. Let's go relax."

"You know, there must be something about this house that prompts women to drop their drawers for the men around here. After all, this is where Luca and I got into trouble when he and I first met. And look where it got me! Maybe you should rethink your moratorium."

"Lightning doesn't strike twice," Taylor said. "Of that we can be sure."

Chapter Fifteen

"WHAT the hell bee flew up your *culo*," Matteo said to his brother Sandro after he shouted at his third contractor in twenty minutes. "We've worked on this thing for how many years and never once do you raise your voice, and now all of a sudden you're turning into Mr. Badass?"

Sandro scrubbed his hands over his beard. "But he should have known better than to put that on that way," he said, pointing to a railing that got screwed in backward.

"Duly noted." He ran his fingers through his wavy, dark hair. "But we're all tired, we've all been under the gun, and there's a lot to finalize here before we have five hundred guests converge on this place tomorrow night."

"Tell me about it," Sandro said. "I'm not even interested in this thing anymore. I just want it to be over."

Matteo scrunched his brow, then placed his palm across his brother's forehead. "You okay, bro? You must have some crazy bad fever to be saying things like that. This is your baby. How could you not be totally excited to introduce it to the world tomorrow?"

Sandro shook his head and sighed. "I'm sure I'll regret admitting this to you 'cause you'll give me a heap of shit for it, but out of freaking nowhere, I've got a woman totally messing with my head."

"Gia again?" he said, his voice rising in alarm. "If so, we need to get the police out here immediately."

Sandro shook his head. "No, it's not Crazy Gia. It's someone else."

"Wait a minute." He held up his finger, pointing it at Sandro. "I thought you swore off women for a while."

"Believe me, I did."

"So then what the hell?"

"What the hell is right," he said as he reached for a table to shift it closer to the window. He leaned his hands on the table, looked out on the horizon, and took in a deep breath. He wasn't serious that he wanted the gala over. But his head was definitely a murky mess, and he hated that. "But you know how it goes. You least expect it, then some annoying woman flies in under the radar and you're totally screwed. Only in this case, I wish I had been screwed."

His brother high-fived him, smiling with relief. "Oh, so that's the problem, man? You tried to get some action and got shut down? And now the chase is on, because what better thrill is there than going after the one who won't put out?"

"Uh, yeah, when I was a teenager maybe. But I'm too old for that. I'm not led around by my dick anymore."

Matteo burst out laughing. "That's a complete crock. If ever I heard one. You'll be led around by that little thing of yours until you're ninety."

Sandro smacked him in the crotch playfully. "Twice as big as that microscopic peanut you're hiding."

"So who is this beauty queen who's got you tied up in knots?"

He winced. "Not actually a beauty queen, but she is gorgeous. And trust me, you don't even want to know what her job is."

"I'm sure she's not a model," his brother said, his warm brown eyes frowning. "Because that would be impossible."

Sandro nodded, his lips pursed. "Maybe not completely impossible."

"Oh no. No. No. No way," Matteo said. "Really, Sandro? Couldn't you find an accountant or a dentist or maybe even a street sweeper? Anyone but a damned model? Have you not learned your lesson?"

"It's not like all models are psychopaths."

"No, but wasn't one enough?"

"It doesn't matter anyhow," Sandro said. "It was a one-off and won't happen again."

"She ditched you then?"

"It wasn't a matter of ditching exactly," he said. "More like she got cold feet. At an inopportune time."

"Okay, that's good news. At least one of you has some common sense then. So you were cut off inconveniently. But it's behind you now, and you don't have to deal with her again. You can just pretend it didn't happen and focus on your work. You're a man: use your compartmentalization skills."

"It's not that simple."

"Of course it is. Don't call her, don't show up at the same nightclubs that she goes to for a while, and then she's gone from your life altogether." He snapped his fingers for emphasis.

"Except she's staying here. As a guest in our home. In the room across the hall from my bedroom."

Matteo squinted at him. "What?"

"She came with Luca and his fiancée. Oh, by the way, did you hear that Luca's getting married, of all the stupid things?"

"We'll get back to Luca. I'm still stuck on this woman sleeping across the hall from you."

"That was my stupid idea," Sandro said. "I was trying to be a good host."

"By banging the houseguests? That doesn't seem like the best way to put some distance between the two of you."

"Gee, you think?" Sandro shook his head. "I'm going to have to push the wardrobe in front of my door before I go to sleep tonight."

"Because she's going to come after you?"

Sandro rolled his eyes. "Of course not. Because I'm going to want to go after her."

"You've got it bad."

"Which is bizarre because I've got entirely no interest in her. Whatsoever."

His brother nodded his head. "Keep trying to convince yourself of that. But in the meantime, why don't you at least move her to another room? We've got plenty of spare bedrooms."

Sandro thought about that for a minute but didn't answer. "So what do you think about Luca getting married?"

"I guess this means you're not moving her to another room?"

"That would be weird. And insulting. It would suggest I have no self-control."

"Have you ever considered that maybe you have no self-control?"

Sandro glared. "I can totally keep it in my pants. This will be a test of willpower. I'm certain I can resist her charms."

"Great," Matteo said. "I'll be waiting in the wings to pick up the pieces when this all goes very wrong."

"I've got it all under control."

"In that case, stop bitching at the workmen and let's keep moving," his brother said, clapping his hands. "We've got a lot to do."

"So does that mean you don't want to discuss losing Luca to the dark side?"

"That means I think you should take my advice and compartmentalize your life." Matteo handed him a clipboard. "Why don't you take over for me going through this punch list, and I'll make sure the railing gets put back on correctly."

"Fine."

"Oh, and Sandro? Here—" His brother pulled his wallet from his back pocket, extracting a condom from it and tossing it to him. "Just in case that epic self-control of yours somehow fails."

Sandro could only throw Matteo a dirty look as he caught the offending item and stuck it in his back pocket.

Chapter Sixteen

"THIS is the most adorable little village I think I've ever seen," Taylor said as the four of them took a traditional *passeggiata,* a uniquely Italian custom where the locals take a leisurely stroll through town at dusk. She and her friends made their way through the *centro storico,* the historic center of Santo Romeo. There of course would have been no Santo Romeo were it not for the Romeo family, so the town and the family and the vineyard were all inextricably tied. "And to think this is the town of your heritage, well, it's just hard to conceptualize having such deep roots like this. A town founded by your ancestors hundreds and hundreds of years ago. How cool is that?"

Sandro shrugged. "I guess it's what I've known my whole life, so it is what it is."

"Trust me, it's an amazing gift to have such abiding connections to a community. I'd have given my eyeteeth for something like this."

"Hey, Tay," Larkin said. "Let's do some window-shopping."

The two women separated from the men to stroll arm in arm while admiring shoes and clothes in the stores they walked past. Luca and Sandro took advantage of the women's distraction to talk shop.

"So you're sure about this engagement?" Sandro said. "You do realize that it means you're stuck with the same woman for the rest of your time on Earth?"

Luca rolled his eyes. "Look, Sandro, I know it's hard

for you to understand. You've just not met the right woman, and so the idea of binding yourself for life is—"

"Is something like climbing to the top of that bell tower," he said, pointing to the top of the cathedral down the road, "and then taking a flying leap from its highest point."

"Way to be a drama queen," Luca said with a chuckle. "Look, I can't explain it to you but to tell you that I'm happiest when we're together and she makes me a better man."

Sandro ran his fingers through his long hair, then shook his head. "You're right. It is hard for me to understand. Like in the same way I can't understand why she'd pick you to begin with." He elbowed his cousin in the ribs.

"So funny I forgot to laugh."

"You boys sure are deep in discussion," Larkin said, looping her arm into Luca's, leaving Sandro the odd man out of the group. Taylor looked at him walking separately from them and gave half a thought to joining him but then thought better of it. The last thing she wanted was to be embarrassed by his rejecting her attempts at being civil. Far better to pretend he wasn't there.

"Just explaining to Sandro why I'm so excited to marry my best friend." He leaned over and kissed her.

"Honestly, do we need to get you two a room?" Taylor said as she jokingly stuck her finger down her throat.

"Yeah, enough with the fondling and making out," Sandro said. "I'm trying to work up an appetite, not lose it."

They laughed as they wandered through the town, admiring the charming buildings made of earthen limestone and warm sandstone facades, their terra-cotta roofs reflecting the honeyed glow of the setting sun. Taylor's gaze scanned the panorama: from the imposing cathedral that had been the anchor of this town since the Renaissance to the tiny open-air market that was closing up shop for the evening.

They arrived at a tiny restaurant and walked through to the back where they were seated at a table on an outdoor terrace overlooking the valley below just in time for sunset. Ribbons of purple and rose streaked the melon sky as the evening gave way to the night sky.

"It's so beautiful," Taylor said, nodding to the colors. "It takes my breath away."

"Nothing like a Tuscan sunset," Sandro said. "It is said that it is in *Toscano* that God perfected his color palette."

"I can believe it," Larkin said. "I've never been here when the sky hasn't been absolutely gorgeous."

"Speaking of gorgeous," Luca said, "You ladies look beautiful tonight."

Taylor knew that comment was aimed at his fiancée, but he was kind enough to ensure she wasn't left feeling outside the group. Not that Taylor was in need of flattery—she spent her life being poked, prodded, and primped by others who fawned over her natural good looks to the point of distraction. Nevertheless, it was always nice to have a handsome man acknowledge it. And clearly Sandro wasn't going to be that man.

"Flattery will get you nowhere with me," Taylor said, laughing.

"Luca's right," Sandro said, fixing his eyes on Taylor's. "You look breathtaking tonight."

Taylor gulped. Breathtaking? Even if she did, how

strange for those words to come from the curmudgeon's mouth. She expected something more along the lines of fire spitting from his tongue. She wondered what his ulterior motive was. Surely he wasn't saying that just to be kind.

"Thank you, Sandro," she said. "Even though that sweet talk won't get you anywhere either."

His face fell, and she no sooner said the words than she realized he had actually been sincere, and she felt awful for being so cynical. "Oh Sandro," she said, placing her hand on his wrist. "I was only joking. I didn't mean for that to be as rude as it must have sounded."

He shook his head. "No worries. It's all good."

But she could sense it wasn't all good, and dinner proceeded with very little interaction between the two of them, with Sandro seeming to address Luca or Larkin exclusively throughout the meal, never Taylor.

They were finishing after-dinner espressos when a woman approached the table.

"I'm so sorry to bother you," she said, looking at Taylor. "But would you mind if I took a quick selfie with you that I could send to my daughter? She thinks you hung the moon, what with being so beautiful and all, but also for your charitable work. She even wrote a paper about all the good works that you've done behind the scenes, for a college seminar she took on volunteering."

Taylor blushed. As used as she was to being the center of attention, it was in small gatherings like this that she still felt awkward being singled out for her looks. But when the woman referenced her philanthropic work, something dearest to her heart, she won her over instantly.

"I'd love to," Taylor said, standing up and grabbing

her phone. Since she was taller with the longest arms, she had the best chance of getting a good shot of the two of them. Taylor wrapped her arm around the woman, extended her arm in front of them, and smiled broadly for the picture.

"I'm so honored," the woman said. "Everyone is going to be so jealous when they see this picture up on my Instagram account!"

Taylor smiled. She felt lucky that it took little effort on her part to make someone else's day. Funny, the only one who seemed mostly immune to her many fine qualities was Alessandro Romeo. Good thing she didn't need him in her life. And vice versa, for that matter.

Chapter Seventeen

SANDRO felt like a damned tennis ball being volleyed back and forth on a bed of hot coals. Every time he resolved to completely not give a care for Taylor McFarland, something would happen to cause him to reconsider his dug-in attitude. And now he overheard from some complete stranger fan-girl woman that Taylor was some sort of superhero philanthropist? It was hard to have that jibe with his preconceived notion that she was your run-of-the-mill narcissistic supermodel. Even though plenty of signs kept pointing elsewhere.

Following dinner, they'd returned to the palazzo and were relaxing on the terrace in front of a large outdoor fireplace, enjoying a reserve Romeo Chianti that Sandro was particularly proud of.

"I must say, Sandro, your family does produce a pretty impressive bottle of wine," Taylor said. "Well, I guess it wouldn't be just a bottle. More like a cask or cellar. Or something like that. Not sure of my wine terminology."

"Thank you," he said. "We've been working on it long enough that we should have it mastered by now. Though of course so many variables go into the end product, many of which are out of our control."

"Any chance we can order enough of this to serve at our wedding?" Larkin said.

Sandro nodded. "I'll be sure to make it happen. Consider it my gift to you both." He gave them a nod and lifted his glass. He was gradually coming around to the fact that this was happening, like it or not. And if he had to lose his good friend to someone, at least it was Larkin, whom he could see was good for Luca.

Larkin stretched her arms and yawned. "I don't know about you folks, but I had a rough day. Between that long, leisurely breakfast; relaxing by the pool all day interrupted only by a long, leisurely lunch; punctuated by a long, leisurely dinner— Well, I'm beat. Not to mention so stuffed."

"Stuffed just like that unbelievable ravioli I ate too much of tonight," Taylor said, rubbing her belly. "I think I've got a food baby in there."

Luca got up and extended his hand to Larkin. "Let's see if we can end the day with a long, leisurely—"

Taylor held up her hands. "Thanks, don't think we need to be privy to that information.

Luca smiled. "I knew that would make you want to get rid of us that much sooner. Good night, you two!"

Taylor felt like that should have been her cue to excuse herself as well, but it was such a beautiful night and such a perfect temperature, she wasn't ready to call it a night. It was still early enough in the summer they were spared the oppressive heat that would soon envelop much of Italy. Once again, the sky was awash with jewellike stars studded across a soft blanket of black. A comfortable breeze stirred up the scent of rosemary, lavender, and sage planted in gardens surrounding the terrace.

Taylor took off her shoes and stretched her long legs out to rest on the low wrought iron and Italian-tiled tabletop in front of them.

"Make yourself right at home," Sandro said, teasing her.

"Don't mind if I do. You okay if I hang out a few more minutes?" she said. "You're perfectly welcome to go to bed. It's just so lovely out here, I hate to turn in early and miss this chance to commune with the night sky for a bit."

"Commune away," he said. "I'm enjoying having a moment's peace before things get crazy tomorrow."

"Do you sort of wish you'd not bothered with the big party and instead just quietly opened the thing?"

He frowned. "In a way maybe. But that's not how my family does things. We're all about the fanfare."

"Speaking of family," she said. "Rumor has it you've got a large one. But I've yet to meet a one of them."

He raised an eyebrow. "Huh. I guess that's true. Mamma's been away. She gets back in town just before things get underway tomorrow. Everyone else has been busy helping to get ready. Some in the office fielding media calls, guest questions, that sort of thing. Others overseeing last-minute finishing touches with things like carpentry. The rest are dealing with the details of the event itself. Come to think of it, I guess I'm the only one who's taken a break over the past few days."

"Is that a good thing or a bad thing in the eyes of your siblings?"

He shrugged. "We're a very egalitarian group here. Each of us contributes plenty to the end result, and none of us resents the other for occasionally putting in a little less effort. Not that I've not put in my own sweat equity with this thing. Believe me, I have in spades."

He reached over for the bottle of wine and refilled their glasses.

"Was this thing your idea then?" She took a sip of her

drink and savored it.

He shook his head vigorously. "No, not at all. This was my father's project originally. He'd wanted so much to see this to fruition. But he never even got it off the ground before he died."

She wrinkled her brow. "I'm so sorry."

He shook his head. "It was a long time ago, although it still feels almost like yesterday. Papà would be so proud of this moment. His family came together to fulfill his dream."

"And you were in charge of it?"

He stood up and put another piece of wood on the fire. Sparks flew as the wood crackled, and the intoxicating aroma of cypress filled the air.

"The day my father died was the day I became a man," he said. "I had no choice. As the oldest of six, someone needed to be in charge. My mother was so filled with grief it was all she could do to be there for us in even a small way. Of course we had help; that is the advantage of having wealth. But no amount of money can replace a man like my papà, who was a good man, an ambitious man with big dreams." He spread out his arms. "Including this."

"Quite a burden for a young man."

"I was about to enter university when he died," he said. "I knew nothing about responsibility."

"It must have been hard. I'm so sorry."

"You don't know the half of it," he said. "My mamma, as I said, was there but not there. My brothers and my sister lashed out and then blamed me for trying to be in charge. My sister Valentina mocked me, calling me papà but not in a good way. She meant that I was bossy and demanding.

"There were many pressures." He stared out across the

vineyard. "I managed the family, I managed the business, I even took classes when I could and eventually earned my degree. And of course this pet project of my father's became my firstborn. It was my goal to take it to fruition."

"Did you ever have time for just you?"

He shook his head. "Certainly not in the early days. When my peers were out sowing their wild oats, I was overseeing the harvest, planning for the next season. Of course, we had many workers who could help with that, but there was much to learn, which left little time for playing."

"Which begs the question: how did you earn your reputation as such a playboy?" she said. "I think Larkin may have mentioned that along the way."

"I fear my image far exceeds my reality," he said, frowning. "But what about you? A famous supermodel and all. No doubt you've been courted by countless men."

She smiled. "Courted. Such a charming word. But no, I wouldn't say I've been courted so much as perpetually hit upon. For some reason men think they can just have a piece of women in my business, which isn't the case. At least with me it's not."

"How did you ever decide to get into modeling anyhow?"

"It helped that I was a human skyscraper, I suppose," she said with a chuckle. "By the time I was in high school, my mother had found a somewhat steady job and we actually lived in a tiny studio apartment. It was a palace. We still had no money though. But when you're that age, your friends always want to go to the mall to shop, right? So I would go to the mall, I just would never buy anything."

"I'm sorry about that," he said. "I think about Valentina at that age, and I can't remember what she was more crazy about: boys or clothes."

"Yeah, well, the boys thing took care of itself since I was too tall for them," she said. "But the mall was our favorite hangout. And one day I was at the mall and a man came up to me and asked me if I'd done any modeling. Of course, I wasn't stupid and didn't just believe the man. But I took his phone number—after laughing out loud at the prospect—and went home and talked to my mom."

"And that was it?"

"Sort of, yeah," she said. "I was under contract a few weeks later, on my way to New York, and never looked back."

"Did you miss your mother?"

"I guess the way I grew up, I was ready to find something better. Sure, I missed her. But I also was pretty darned happy to have a job that paid great money. No more struggling, no more scrimping, no more hardship. No more enduring poverty."

He clapped. "Brava. A happy ending finally."

"Mostly so. You're right about that," she said. "Though with fame has come the need to circle the wagons. I had to learn to be very wary, particularly of men. Sometimes it seems that everyone wants to be your friend and every man wants a piece of you. Eventually I learned to not put myself in the position of being hurt by men who wanted to use me. It's a hard lesson to learn, but it's okay—we all have to learn that to some degree, don't we?"

"This is true. Sometimes you trust, and it ends up burning you. Or your beloved car," he added under his breath.

"Huh?"

"Oh, nothing."

Red-Hot Romeo

They sat for a while in silence but for the crackle of the fire and the sounds of the night.

"The peacefulness of this is enticing," she said. "You are very spoiled living here."

"You're right. I am. Though I have deep appreciation for my connection to this place, the land beneath our feet, and all that the earth pushes forth. It's a part of me, and I'm a part of it."

"I envy you that connection."

"But surely with your great success you have some amazing penthouse apartment that you now call home."

"Actually, I bought my mother a home for her very own when I hit it big," she said. "But it didn't make sense for me to spend the money on something for me since I'm on the road so often. When I travel I stay at the nicest hotels, so I'm not suffering. But it does mean I'm not planted anywhere in particular. I guess everywhere is home for me now. Which isn't a bad thing: the world is an amazing place, and I've had the chance to see a lot of it."

"I have a feeling you'll end up right where you're meant to be someday," he said. "And when it happens, you'll appreciate that it's home more than just about anyone."

She nodded. "Maybe by then I can come back here and buy you out." She laughed.

"I'm afraid you'd have to take that up with a whole lot of Romeos," he said. "And there's strength in numbers."

"In that case, maybe I can buy a small parcel of land nearby that can be my own. I really love it here. Something about it speaks to me."

Only the more she talked to this red-hot Romeo, the more she knew that would likely not be such a good plan.

She could resist him for the duration of a short weekend getaway, but forever? She doubted she had the stamina to withstand him for that long. For that matter, she could feel her defenses weakening with every shared word between them. She knew she needed to extricate herself before she did something stupid.

"Thanks for a great evening, Sandro," she said, getting up and reaching down for her sandals. "And thanks for staying up with me and sharing your thoughts. Seems you're not such a bad guy after all."

He frowned. "Gee, thanks for the ringing endorsement. Turns out you're not such a bad supermodel yourself." He chucked her on the shoulder as she turned to head to bed.

And she walked into the house, wishing she were brave enough to set aside her fears and show him what kind of supermodel she really was, so to speak. But she wasn't willing to risk it; her heart was too fragile to take such a crazy chance.

Chapter Eighteen

IT took all Sandro's willpower to not chase after Taylor as she walked away from him. Especially after he got a nice peek down her top when she leaned over to grab her shoes. Oh well, clearly it just wasn't meant to be—he was far too proud to beg. Instead, he opted to sit outside and indulge in the solitude his life rarely afforded him. If he couldn't have a gratuitous little fling, at least he could enjoy a few moments of uninterrupted peace and quiet.

He was surprised to see this side of Taylor. She seemed like a nice woman, no pretenses, just going about her life, minding her business and lending a helping hand to others. He had to respect that about the woman.

After about half an hour, he took a final sip of his wine, checked that the embers were dying in the fireplace, and finally retreated to bed. He had a crazy busy day ahead of him, and he badly needed some shut-eye.

Sandro was in a deep, deep sleep when he heard a knock on his door. At first it seemed like it was just part of his dream, but it grew louder and louder until it finally jarred him awake.

He jumped out of bed and opened the door, stark naked, to see Taylor standing before him, ashen-faced and panting wildly like she'd just seen a ghost.

"What's wrong?"

"S-s-s-snake." She pointed toward her room. "There's a snake. In there."

"Is this part of your bad dreams?"

"No," she said loudly. "This is not a bad dream. This is a wide-awake nightmare. There is a snake. In there. Now."

"Impossible. We might have snakes out on the farm but never in the house."

She kept pointing to the room, her face white. "I'm telling you there's a big damned snake in there."

"How did you find a snake if you were asleep?"

"I woke up again," she said. "I had a bad dream so I woke up. I'd left a window open to let the cool night air in, but the sheer curtains were drawn. I went over to open them to look out at the sky. I wanted to try to see the Milky Way. So I walked over to the window, and there it was, coiled on the window seat as if it belonged there. It's a snake, I'm telling you."

Sandro wondered for a minute if the woman had completely lost it. A snake? In her bedroom? He'd sooner expect to see a porcupine or a wild boar in there.

Without thinking, he approached her room and entered.

"Don't turn on the light," she said in a hushed voice. "You don't want him to charge. Or strike. Or whatever they do."

99

He slowly approached the window, and there was enough moonlight streaming in that he saw it as plain as day: a fat, coiled viper, acting as if he owned the place.

He looked at Taylor. "You were right. There's a snake in your room."

She hit her forehead with the heel of her hand. "Oh gee, you think? What are we going to do about it?"

"Calm down. I know what to do with it, I just never had to do this in the house before. Let me get down to the toolshed and I'll get the snake tongs. Give me a few minutes."

"Snake tongs?" she said. "Are you planning to sauté the thing?"

He laughed. "No, they'll just help me get a grip on it so I can haul it away. You stay right here, and I'll be back as soon as possible."

She followed behind him. "I'm not staying in here waiting for you, buster."

"Fine," he said. "Then come on. I need to get back to sleep or I'm going to be a mess tomorrow."

They left the room together, and as they reached the hallway, he looked down, realizing he'd been completely naked the whole time. He looked up just in time to see her lifting her gaze back up as well.

"So there's that," he said.

"Ummmm." She averted her gaze—but only after he'd caught her staring and licking her lips.

"Yeah. Mind if I take care of this?"

"By all means. I think that would be best," she said, nervously rolling back on her heels, extending her arm toward his room. "I'll wait here."

He returned within a minute wearing a pair of Puma

soccer shorts slung low across his abdomen, which she promptly stared at.

He pointed at her skimpy pajamas. "You sure you don't want to find something a little more decent to wear in case we run into anyone?" His concern was more for the hard-on that was going to pop up any minute, more likely the longer he stared at her in that outfit.

"I'll take my chances," she said. "'Cause I'm not going in there for anything."

"Then let's go." He grabbed her hand and pulled her down the corridor, out through the terrace doors, and down toward the farm. They ran for a few minutes till they reached a large stone shed where Sandro made her stay outside. He didn't want to risk a chance encounter with a snake in the shed as well, although he didn't dare tell her that. He grabbed the tool, a snake hook, as well as a five-gallon bucket, then returned to her, and they raced back to the main house together.

They were breathing heavily as they returned to the room.

Sandro turned to her. "You ready?"

"Me?" she said, leaning over with her hands on her knees, catching her breath. "You're the one who needs to be ready. Are you sure you know what you're doing? This seems like you should call an expert for something this dangerous. Because if you get bitten, I'm so going to kill you!"

"So you'd kill me if I got myself killed then?"

"Exactly."

"The thing is," he said, "you've got a job to do with me."

"If you mean you want me to pray for you, I'm all in."

"I mean you're going to use this," he said, handing her the hook.

"Are you freaking crazy? I know absolutely nothing about snake handling. And point of fact, I don't even like snakes."

"Then that's good, because you're not going to have to become best friends with the thing," he said. "You're just going to keep that tail under control while I gently clamp up toward the head. I'll be in charge of all the scary things, okay?"

"What else scary is there to do?"

"I need to quickly get the lid on after we drop him into the bucket. And hope he doesn't strike."

"Oh crap. Oh crap. Oh crap. Oh crap."

"Okay, so take a deep breath," he said, rubbing her shoulders and giving her a little pep talk. "You can do this."

She shook out her arms as if she were preparing for an Olympic swim. "Okay. I can do this." She turned her head to each shoulder, an athlete preparing for the event of a lifetime.

Sandro turned the knob and opened the door. Luckily, the snake was still curled up on the window seat. Sandro nodded to her. "Just follow my instructions, and this will be easy."

She rolled her eyes. "I feel like maybe I should just put my wrist in front of him and get the bloodletting over with: let him pierce that forked tongue into my artery and call it a day."

They slowly approached the snake. "It's actually quite beautiful with that dark brown zigzag band on his back. Beautifully designed for camouflage."

"Just what I needed, a beautiful snake that I wouldn't

have seen until the thing bit me."

Sandro placed the bucket with the lid on the floor nearby, got the tongs ready, and before the snake even knew what was happening, he had lowered the tongs to trap it. "Now Taylor, you're just going to use that hook to sort of guide the tail in case it starts moving. You just want to guide it to where we want it, which is right where it is. It's going to remain horizontal as long as we keep it on a horizontal surface. But when I pick this thing up, it's going to want to move upward. You just make sure to keep his tail sort of staying in place while I get him into the bucket. On the count of three: one, two, three."

With the precision of a skilled serpent tamer, he maneuvered the snake into the tub, and Taylor performed her duties as flawlessly as possible all things considered. She might or might not have squealed at one point as Sandro screwed the lid onto the bucket.

And then Sandro threw down the tongs and high-fived Taylor. "Look at you, you snake charmer you! You did it!"

Taylor heaved a sigh. "You were the brave one, Sandro. I could never have done that. Oh my God, when you put that thing on his neck—or whatever you call it. That was amazing. I have newfound respect for you!"

He threw her a look. "I'm not sure if I should take that as a compliment, but I will."

"Believe me, it is."

They walked out to the hallway with the snake tools and the bucket with the offending home invader.

"You okay now?" he said, rubbing her back. "I'll take care of making sure this never ever returns to our home again. Why don't you go ahead and get back to sleep now that you're safe?"

"You sure you'll be okay with that creature?"

He nodded. "I'm fine." It was going to be a while till Sandro could get back to bed, but it didn't make sense for both of them to remain awake.

She stretched up on tiptoes and gave him a quick kiss on his forehead. "Thanks for saving me, Sandro."

At least for a few minutes, he was no longer cranky Sandro in her eyes and instead became the hero. He hated to admit it, but he could definitely get used to that.

Chapter Nineteen

TAYLOR stood in the hallway for a few minutes watching Sandro's back—his strong, tan back punctuated by a particularly gorgeous-looking ass—as he carried the snake bucket and implements far, far away (she hoped). She turned to go back into her room but then thought better of it.

There had been a big, fat, venomous snake sharing her room only a few short minutes ago. What if snakes were like ants, or mice, and it just meant there was more than one? How would she know? Plus she'd left the window open, darn it. Maybe snakes were slithering in at that very minute as she stood there contemplating her sleeping options.

Oh God. She couldn't sleep in there! She'd lie in that bed waiting for the snakes to come murder her in her sleep. Even while she was awake. Because she couldn't sleep! In case there were snakes.

She tried to use a rational mind. Think of the snakes like those scary cadaver men surrounding her car in her dreams. They weren't even real. It was all a concoction of her vivid imagination. She shuddered. She could not sleep in that room. At least not until someone went through it with a fine-tooth comb. Or snake tongs. Whatever it took. A snake eradication expert. She stared up and down the hall, not knowing what to do. She could go find a living room and try to sleep on a sofa. But this house was full of look-don't-touch rooms, certainly not designed for

bedroom-less vagrants to park themselves in.

There were all sorts of other rooms down this hallway, possibly all empty and in need of an occupant. But doors were closed. What if she walked in on someone sleeping? What if it was one of his brothers, having sex with his wife? Oh God, she didn't even know if his brothers were married or not. He could just be having sex with his girlfriend. Or what if it was his sister with some guy she met at a nightclub. The last thing she'd want would be for Taylor to show up and catch them in the act. Or his grieving widowed mother. No, that would be hugely embarrassing.

She looked at her door, then she looked at Sandro's door, then back to hers again. No. There was only one option: she made an executive decision on the spot that she was going to sleep in Sandro's room.

She turned and reached for his doorknob but paused before she turned it. What if there was someone else in there? Not like she'd seen him with anyone since she'd gotten there, but still. Maybe he had a booty call in there. *Oh please, that's nuts. You were with him until just an hour or two ago.* Okay, so maybe no booty call in there. But it was his domain. Would he be angry that she took it upon herself to invade his space? Surely he'd be a grown-up about it and understand. After all, she was a veritable damsel in distress.

She turned the knob, entered the room, and flicked on the light switch. In contrast to the historical design of the rest of the house, his room was unexpectedly contemporary: three walls were a soft dove gray, and the wall behind the bed was black. The wall in front of the bed had a large flat-screen television mounted to it. The carpet was a shade darker than the walls, and his bed was dressed in sleek, gray sheets and a comforter just a tinge darker still, with a leather headboard also in gray. Very modern black leather furniture—a footstool, a reading chair, a love seat— was scattered about.

Unfortunately, the love seat wasn't nearly big enough for a tall girl like herself to be able to sleep on without having to curl into a pretzel. She stared at the bed: would it be acceptable for her to just slip beneath the sheets when he wasn't looking? How rude would she be to take it upon herself to do that? But then she remembered: these were extremely extenuating circumstances. She nearly died tonight. Ish. The least he could do was yield to her a miniscule sliver of bed. If need be, she'd make herself impossibly tiny, the way mice do when they crawl through teensy little holes. He'd hardly even notice she was there.

She was right: this was the sensible thing to do. Just snuggle on in, cross her fingers that she picked the right side of the bed, the one he didn't sleep on, and hope for the best.

So she padded to the far side of the bed, hedging her bets that he would normally just pass out at the closest dropping point nearest the door. She lifted up that comfortable-looking down blanket, and she slipped beneath the crisp, percale sheets, not even letting herself worry about what other women might have been in this bed before and if the man had even washed his sheets in the past five years. He had maids; she knew she was safe.

Sandro was doomed to be a zombie at the launch of his ten-years-in-the-making baby. He'd resigned himself to it already. It was out of his control. Who'd have thought a damned snake would be the source of his woes? If he was going to get no sleep after a visit to Taylor's room, he'd have hoped it would be for something more personal—and personally gratifying—than getting rid of a venomous viper. Just his luck, the way things had been going lately.

As he walked to his room, he glanced over at Taylor's door. He had a half a mind to check on her, just to make sure she was all right. But it would have been awkward for him to just open the door and walk in unannounced. He figured she was fine or he'd have heard about it by now. She'd proven that she was perfectly willing to use that voice of hers if need be.

He entered his room, not even bothering to turn on the light. Padding to the bed, he quickly stripped off his shorts and slipped underneath the sheets. Feeling restless, he reached above his head and bunched his pillow, then pulled it toward his head. Man, he needed to sleep. Badly. He closed his eyes, reflecting on the events of the night. Damn, they were all lucky that snake had decided to settle down right by the window. Imagine if poor Taylor had found the thing in her bed. She'd have been dead of a heart attack long before that snake could have gotten to her. He felt so bad; never had anyone ever found a snake inside the house. What a crazy thing to have happen, tonight of all nights.

He rolled to his side, but as he drifted off to sleep, he could swear he heard the quiet breathing of a sleeping human. What the hell? He sat up, his eyes adjusting to the dark. He could barely make out a lump on the far side of the bed. He reached for his phone on the nightstand, and instead of turning on the too-bright flashlight, he opened the home screen, which afforded him just enough light to see what—or who—was there without causing a commotion.

He saw a passed-out Taylor, curled up on the farthest edge of the bed, practically on the verge of falling off, snoring softly with each intake of breath. She must have been too scared to sleep in her room but too embarrassed to admit it when they were standing in the hallway. Sort of cute of her really.

He stared at her for a few minutes, wanting so badly to run his fingers through her soft blond curls. And then maybe let his hands wander a little lower. But he knew that would be a violation of trust. She was comfortable enough to have opted to sleep in his bed; he owed it to her to respect her space.

Because of course he would have one of the world's most beautiful women sleeping practically on top of him, forbidden fruit that he could, under no circumstances, touch. Sometimes life was so unfair.

Chapter Twenty

TAYLOR woke to the sensation of warm breath on her neck. Had she fallen asleep next to a dog?

She opened her eyes to a darkened room, and it took a minute for the events of the previous night to return to her. She'd gone to sleep. In Sandro's bed. So no dog next to her, rather it was Sandro whose breath fluttered against her flesh. She no sooner realized that than she noticed something even more surprising. Not only was he breathing on her neck, but also his right arm and leg were draped across her waist and thigh, and unless she was sorely mistaken, she felt another appendage also cozying itself right up against her behind.

Well. This was quite the dilemma. Awkward sleeping circumstance number 264 or something like that: what to do when you wake up in a man's bed uninvited, only to find the man there. As in *there*.

She lay there for what seemed like forever, the soft chuff of his warm breath feeling kind of reassuring against her skin as she tried to figure out the best way to handle the situation. On the one hand, she had plunked herself down uninvited last night. But then again, she didn't have a chance to clear it with him beforehand and was forced to make an executive decision. But only because he was doing her a solid with that slithering, scale-covered death squad that had invaded her space.

Under the circumstances, she knew she didn't have a right to be indignant right now. But how best to extricate herself from his warm, very hot body? And by hot, she meant *hot*. She thought back to last night when he raced to her aid. And there he stood, nothing on but what the good Lord gave him. If she hadn't been so freaked out about the venomous intruder in her midst, she wouldn't have minded focusing on that little gift for a while longer.

It wasn't often you got to see six plus feet of incredibly sexy Italian and all the accoutrements that come with that, just right there for your viewing pleasure. She made a mental inventory of him from top to bottom: she loved when a man kept his hair a little long, and his was just the right length, long enough to pull back and run your fingers through when— Well, suffice it to say, run your fingers through. And that sexy little goatee—she kept remembering what it felt like to kiss him, with that soft hair pressed to her lips, and couldn't help but wonder how it would feel scraping across her skin. Not to mention elsewhere. Working her way down his hard body, remembering his strong arms with biceps that looked like they came from hard work, then that beautiful chest with just the right amount of hair on it to make it sexy. And following that hair along his six-pack abs to her most favorite zone of all, that impossible-to-resist path of hair that led right where every red-blooded woman with a libido wanted to go. It made her heart beat faster just thinking about that little Hansel and Gretel trail.

Get a grip, Taylor. But it was hard to get a grip because she wanted him. Damn, was that totally hypocritical of her? So maybe she'd had a change of heart, but wasn't that a woman's prerogative to do just that? Besides, hadn't he shown himself to be a man of integrity? He seemed thoughtful, and kind, and generous. What harm would

there be in exploring things with him? Or at the very least exploring *him* with things: like her mouth, her lips, her tongue?

She pressed her backside up closer to him, pulled his hand tight to her breast, and drifted off to sleep, figuring she'd let the chips fall where they would.

Sandro emerged from what felt like a coma of exhaustion, slowly opening his eyes in the dark room only to find himself nestled perfectly belly-to-back against a warm, soft body. And unless he was mistaken, wasn't that his hand pressed up to a warm, soft breast? He groaned and moved closer to Taylor, trying in his foggy mind to make sense of what he was encountering and how he'd gone from not having a chance in hell with the woman to being close enough to being able to slip it right in without her even noticing. At least not initially. Though he'd hope that soon enough she'd gratefully applaud the maneuver and not want to cut off his balls.

So he knew this: it wasn't the first night when things unfolded so unexpectedly and then he was unceremoniously voted out of the tribe. But then the second night, what happened then? It was starting to come back to him: he went to bed, late. He was super exhausted.

And then the snake— Oh, that blessedly perfect little snake. So that's what he owed his great good fortune to. Shame he'd dropped that viper down a ravine twenty minutes away from here, or he'd go reward the thing with a tasty rat for his efforts, maybe even name one of his wines after him.

He pulled Taylor closer to his body, subtly pressing his erection into the soft pillow of her ass. And of course he groaned. How could he not? He decided to go big or go home, so he pressed his lips to the nape of her neck, alternating small kisses and gentle licks as his right hand got busy toying with Taylor's already-hard nipple. Was he imagining this? Or was it really happening?

Wait a minute. The snake. Maybe he'd actually been bitten by the snake. And maybe he died. And maybe now right now he was in heaven, and in heaven—God help us all—you're permanently hard and raring to go with a ready and willing female curled up in front of you at all times! Would that be possible? He reached down with his left hand and pinched hard on his hip, just to see if he'd notice it. Because if it hurt, surely then it would mean he was alive. After all, no one feels pain in heaven, right?

He winced at the feel of it. Crap, that was maybe too hard.

Okay, so he wasn't dead. That was a good sign. And Taylor, right in front of him, was decidedly warm and alive. Now he had to simply figure out how to navigate the treacherous body of water known as Taylor McFarland without drowning. Or being decimated by sharks or other predatory creatures. Piece of cake.

As he nestled in a bit closer, his mouth found her ear, and he ever so stealthily licked and kissed it while his hand

slid beneath her wifebeater—ah, that gloriously skimpy T-shirt he remembered so fondly from his first failed attempt—and then back toward her breast, swirling his palm on her belly as he moved his hand upward.

"Don't stop," Taylor moaned, and he took it as tacit approval as his palm spread across her breast and squeezed.

Sandro was forever grateful that she hadn't shunned his advances—yet—because he didn't think he'd survive tonight if he were left dangling—make that jutting out—again. It would be a particular form of torture he wasn't prepared to survive. Instead, he opted for bravery, slowly inching his body so that he could move his mouth toward hers, which meant no more spooning, boohoo, but with any luck could result in even greater riches. He soon maneuvered Taylor so that she was on her back, giving him much greater access, and he took advantage of that, slipping his hand beneath the elastic band of her bikini panties and *oh God, oh God, oh God.*

Nirvana, he thought as his fingers glided through her slickness. If there had been any question about whether this was arousing her as much as him, at least now he had answers. He swirled his fingers, pressing in deeper till he could thrust first one then two fingers inside her. And just when he thought he'd died and gone to heaven—snake-free—she reached for him and wrapped her hands around his erection, and he thought he'd not be able to hold it, it felt so perfect, her warm hands stroking him in just the right tempo.

In the darkness, his mouth found hers and their tongues met, tasting, stroking, twining, as their hands busily pulled and rubbed and stroked. Taylor let out tiny sounds of pleasure that made him want to cry out with joy, but he was too busy trying to keep from coming and ending this little surprise party too soon. He was trying to think what he'd done to deserve this, but he couldn't concentrate long enough to even care, focused as he was on her hands, exploring his cock and his balls and oh God, he was going to explode any second.

He pulled her panties down, rolling off her for one minute to reach for his nightstand drawer—the freebie condom from his brother being too far to access. He pulled out a condom, tore the packet with his teeth, and rolled it on himself in record time.

They were both breathing hard now, Taylor thrusting her hips as soon as he moved his hands back down there. In the dark it felt amazing, as if it honed all his senses, the sound of their moaning, the smell of her arousal, the taste of her mouth, the feel of her slick juices on his fingers. He couldn't wait another second and rolled so he was on top of her, and finally they were chest-to-chest, her breasts rubbing against his own nipples, and he thought he would die from the pleasure.

He spread her legs with his knees and positioned his cock at her center. "You sure about this?" he whispered between kisses. He didn't want her to experience buyer's remorse once they went down this path. Even if it was just going to be for a night, it was going to be mutually agreeable and they would both walk away with no regrets.

She nodded, licking his lips. "Put it in me now, or I might just change my mind."

He could feel her smiling against his mouth. "Your wish is my command," he said as he slowly eased himself into her, savoring the feel of her tightness around him.

Once he seated himself deep inside her, he grabbed

her knees and spread her legs wide as he began to move with purposeful strokes: in, out, in, out. Taylor wrapped her legs around him, and he leaned forward to catch her nipple in his mouth as their bodies met then separated, his movements getting faster, his cock impossibly harder. He reached a hand down between them and rubbed her just there, right where he knew she needed it, occasionally stretching fingers to feel where their bodies were joined, which made him wild with pleasure. His mind went fuzzy, so focused was he on homing in on the warmth of her body, the glide of his cock as it pressed into her, the squeeze of her body as it closed around him. He bit softly on her nipple as he buried himself to the hilt, finally letting loose with wave after wave of spasms just as she joined him, her muscles clamping down on him as he came hard, then collapsed in her arms.

If how it began was any indication, this was gonna be a great day.

Chapter Twenty-One

MAYBE it wasn't fair to compare, being that it had been a long damned time since she'd slept with anyone. But wow. That was like nothing she'd ever experienced before. Making love with Sandro felt like so much more than just sex: it felt like some mystical bond, some unspoken connection that she didn't understand but wanted to explore more of.

As she lay there in the dark, just feeling, simply experiencing Sandro's body exploring hers, she felt like she'd known him, known this feeling, her whole life. He stroked his hands along her body, drew his tongue across the nape of her neck, pressed his fingers inside her slick body. The sensual pleasure of being half-asleep while being aroused was downright amazing. Thank goodness she'd decided to stop being a twit and go for it. Because that, beyond a shadow of a doubt, was worth it.

They lay together, spent, breathing heavily and not saying a word for long minutes.

Finally Sandro rolled off her, lying on his side propped up on his elbow, facing her in the dark room, continuing to skirt his hands all over her body as if he didn't want to let go, not even for a second. He reached over and twirled her hair in his fingers. "Lucky me, finding Goldilocks sleeping in my bed."

Taylor smiled. "I hope you don't mind. I was too scared to return to my room last night."

"Mind?" he said, incredulous. "Are you kidding? That

was the best gift I could have ever found after a night of hardship."

"Hardship? I didn't realize talking beneath the stars with yours truly was such work for you." She reached up to kiss him.

"The talking, all good. The snake, well, that was a different story altogether."

"Yeah. What is up with your allowing snakes in your house?"

"Well, if you hadn't left a personal invitation to the thing," he said. "Did you leave a trail of baby mice that led to your room? I bet this was all part of your master plan to trap me and lure me into your bed."

"Except that I'm in your bed." She tweaked his nose.

"Good point."

"But now that you've got me here," she said. "Good luck getting rid of me. I quite liked the sneak-attack approach."

He leaned over and kissed her before lifting her T-shirt over her head. "I aim to please," he said, kissing his way down her throat, past her collarbone, finding his way to her nipple and securing his lips around it. Taylor moaned as she scraped her fingers through his hair, then dragged her fingernails along his back in a circular motion.

"I could do this all day." She worked her leg between his to press it against his growing erection.

"I could do it all week," he said with a groan. "Too bad reality is soon to encroach on our fun time."

"Awww. Can't we have a couple more minutes?" She moved her foot up to press the top of it against his cock.

"A couple of minutes, absolutely," he said. "How do you want it?"

She pulled him up and rolled him over so that she was on top. "This time I'm in charge." She leaned over to reach for another condom, then shifted down his body, placing kisses along that trail of hair that led her to the prize. Clasping his cock in her hand, she stroked her tongue up and around and back down again before spreading her lips over it.

Sandro moaned loudly.

"You like that?" she said between licking and sucking him.

"Don't. Ever. Stop," he said between gasps, thrusting himself into her mouth.

She looked up at him in the dark. "But I thought we were in a hurry."

He turned to look at the clock. As dark as the room was, it was already approaching nine o'clock. They actually were in a hurry. He had his work cut out for him today. He reached beneath her arms and pulled her up. "Until I can trap you in my lair indefinitely, we need to resort to more timely efforts. He lifted her onto his cock, and she slid down him until they were pelvis to pelvis.

"My God, that's perfection," she said in a whisper, and then she began to ride him, grinding her hips in a circular motion and rising off him, then plunging back down. Sandro lay there, his fingers lazily playing with her nipples while Taylor did the heavy lifting.

"That's it, *carissimo*," he said, encouraging her. "Oh God, *mio amore, si, si*, faster."

The more he whispered to her in Italian, the more turned on she was. Taylor rode him, her body seemingly with a mind of its own, pumping and thrusting until she felt a tingling sensation start deep in her pelvis and spread in

waves as she came long and hard. When she finished, Sandro flipped her over, sliding into her from behind. It didn't take long for him to get there as he clung to her hips while thrusting into her wet body, yelling out her name as he came.

The perfect way to start the day yet again.

Chapter Twenty-Two

LARKIN and Luca had just sat down to breakfast when Taylor showed up.

"Don't you look happy this morning," Larkin said when she saw Taylor smiling from ear to ear.

"What?" Taylor said.

Larkin shrugged. "Oh, nothing. You just look like you're in a good mood. Like if you could whistle you would."

Taylor wrinkled her brow. "I can whistle."

"They why don't you?"

"Um, because I don't have any desire to. Why? Should I?"

"No, silly," Larkin said. "I was just teasing you. I guess it was just wishful thinking since you and Sandro seemed to be enjoying each other's company when we went off to bed."

Yeesh, if only they knew how much they'd enjoyed each other's company. Luckily, she and Sandro had decided to keep that under their hats for now.

Taylor laughed. "That you even noticed that is rather funny considering the two of you seemed a little focused on your own intentions."

Larkin blushed. "Well..."

"Yeah, well," Taylor said. "What's for breakfast, folks?" She smiled the biggest, fakest smile she could, just to throw them off the scent.

Because she and Sandro decided to keep their little

situation under wraps, it meant Taylor couldn't say anything about the snake, which was a bit of a challenge since the incident pretty much defined the past six hours of her life.

"So, we have a hard day of sunbathing in store for us?" Taylor said as the maid served her a cappuccino.

Larkin pretended to yawn. "Yeah, well, it's a tough job, but someone's got to do it. I think Luca's planning to do some heavy lifting with the guys though. He'd feel bad not helping out with anything if they needed him."

"Aww," Taylor said. "I'm totally happy to help out as well. I asked if there was anything we could do, but Sandro declined."

"Oh really?" Larkin said, lifting a brow in curiosity. "When did you do that?"

"Stop, weirdo," Taylor said. "I've offered many times over the past couple of days. I feel bad lounging poolside like a lazybones while they're working hard."

"Yeah, but don't forget we'll take extra long to get ready, so it's not as if we have a carefree day ahead of us." She laughed. "Don't you love hearing me, of all people, saying such a stupid thing?" Before Larkin had met Taylor, she wasn't one to give a care about how she looked, but Taylor had helped her gain an interest in fashion and taught her how best to emphasize her strengths.

Taylor grinned. "Now we just have to figure out what to do until then."

"I say a little food, a little wine," Larkin said.

"I could hardly argue with you," Taylor said. "After all when in Rome... or Tuscany for that matter."

Sandro stopped in while the women were enjoying their lunch poolside.

"Taylor, are you still on call for a little last-minute help?"

"Of course," she said. "I'd love to contribute. What can I do?"

"I need you to run into town for me if you could. The caterer sent everyone ahead, and then her car died on her. I just need you to go to her restaurant and grab her and the remaining things she needs to bring along." He handed her the keys to his car. "My car is parked in front of the house. Just do me a favor and take it really slow."

She nodded. "Okay…," she said, not knowing what that meant.

"Want me to come too?" Larkin asked.

"Sorry, Lark," Sandro said. "There won't be any room in the car once everything is loaded in. You okay with that?"

"Yeah, sure," she said. "I can work on my tan a little longer."

"*Perfetto*," Sandro said. "Elisabetta is waiting for you now, so if you could get a move on, that would be great."

Taylor was dying to talk more, to find out how his morning had gone, to see if everything was shaping up for the party, but she didn't dare for fear of Larkin picking up

on the vibe. She threw on a sarong and slid into her wedge sandals, then walked up to the garden at the front of the house.

Funny how much had changed since the three of them pulled into that parking area a few short nights ago. Damn, things could change in the blink of an eye. Not that she was anticipating anything life-altering between her and Sandro, but if nothing else, what a fantastic weekend it'd been and promised to be still.

She took one look at the only car there and shit a brick.

"Oh no," she said out loud. "Uh-uh. No way. I'm not touching that thing."

Before her was a brand-new Lamborghini Huracán sports coupe. And there was no way in hell she was going to try to figure out how to drive that thing. She'd rather hop on a horse and ride into town. Or hitchhike. Plan B would be Uber, and she grabbed for her phone and saw she had one whopping bar. She hoped for the best as she entered her request for a ride. She didn't want to insult Sandro by refusing to drive his veritable spaceship of a vehicle. This way Sandro would be none the wiser, but she would be a lot less stressed and not responsible for the demise of a very expensive car.

Her Uber driver, a woman named Liliana, arrived in no time flat and was happy to chat with her the entire drive into town. "So you're staying with the Romeos, are you?"

"Yes, I'm a guest of Sandro Romeo—he asked me to fetch Elisabetta since her car broke down."

The driver arched her brow. "Ahh, so you're with Sandro then?"

Taylor, not picking up the nuance, nodded.

"Huh. Strange that he'd have someone new so soon," the woman said. "Considering how awful he was to Gia, leaving her standing at the altar like that."

Taylor squinted at her. "I'm sorry, my Italian isn't that great. Did you say that Sandro left someone at the altar?"

The woman nodded. "It was incredibly cruel," she said. "Her name is Gia. She's a famous model, and she loved him to the depths of her soul. She wanted nothing but the best for him."

"Really?" Taylor said, curious. "Why did he break up with her?"

"It's hard to say really," she said. "I heard she was pregnant and Sandro didn't want to be a father. But then I heard too that he just got bored with Gia and got rid of her."

"But on their wedding day?"

The woman shrugged. "It happens. Someone told me he had another woman lined up. It was all over the tabloids. I hear he's quite the player."

Taylor's brow knit. Quite the player. She'd heard that line before about him. But where had she heard it? It looked like where there was smoke there was fire.

Now that she thought about it, she had heard rumors of some guy named Alessandro, she just hadn't made the connection. A model named Gia had been telling everyone that he'd burned her pretty badly. Taylor wasn't aware that he'd left her high and dry at the altar though. Not to mention possibly pregnant. Wow. From what Taylor had heard at Fashion Week in Paris, the guy had been keeping someone on the side, and Gia heard about it. Gia said that instead of apologizing to her, he'd conspired to get the police involved just to tarnish her name and make her go

away. Now it was all making sense. Alessandro—Sandro—wasn't quite the nice guy she'd been led to believe. Seems instead he was a complete jerk.

"Oh well, I don't know anything about that," Taylor said. "I'm just a houseguest visiting for the weekend. I hardly even know the man."

Except in the biblical sense, but that was going to change *prontissimo*. She was not going to be some patsy that he would use and abuse and ditch like he had with this Gia woman. No, thank you. She was in a drama-free zone in her life and intended to keep it that way.

Chapter Twenty-Three

TAYLOR, dressed in a stunning formfitting metallic silver halter evening gown with a slit to her hip was putting the finishing touches on her makeup when she heard a knock on her door. She was still a bit squeamish about being in the snake room, as beautiful as it was, but she now had no choice: no way was she going to bed down with someone as heartless as Sandro. It was a good thing she hadn't gotten too invested in things with him; easier to cut the cord now before things got too intense.

She opened the door to see Sandro standing before her in a tuxedo. God, he looked so damned amazing. There were some men who were born to be in tuxedos, and Alessandro Romeo was one of them. For a second he took her breath away, standing before her in his black Brioni tux and crisp white shirt, looking like an Italian James Bond. But then she remembered she was not going to play his game.

"*Cara mia,*" he said, reaching for her. "You look stunning." He leaned in to give her a kiss, but she turned her head away so his lips only caught her hair. He frowned, his brows knit in concern. "Is everything okay?"

"Look, Sandro," she said. "I don't want to talk about it now. We can save it for later. Let's just pretend that this morning never happened. Please, go have a lovely time this evening, and I'll be sure to steer clear of you all night."

He grabbed her wrist. "Taylor, why this sudden change of heart? Things were fine at lunchtime."

She shook her head. "I need to finish getting ready, and I'm sure someone needs you somewhere. Why don't you go find them and don't worry about me?"

He tried to clasp her hands in his, but she turned away.

"Thanks, Sandro," she said. "It's been an interesting weekend."

As she closed the door, she pressed her body against it. She knew she was doing the right thing, but why did it feel like it was the completely wrong thing to do?

"This is truly spectacular," Taylor said to Larkin as they wandered through the Romeo Wines headquarters. The space was quickly filling with hundreds upon hundreds of guests, and Luca had offered to give them a tour before things got too crowded.

"I guess I should have shown you the medieval cellars in the palazzo just to have a point of comparison," he said.

The two women shrugged. From where they hailed, they knew no difference between a wine basement from the Middle Ages and any old basement with a washer and dryer and beat-up old pool table.

"Sorry, sweetie," Larkin said. "Perhaps it's a touch of ignoramus American in us. But please, educate us. We're all ears."

"Okay, so you know Alessandro is the principle of the world-famous Cantine dei Marchesi Romeo, makers of some of the best Chiantis Italy has to offer," he said.

"I believe we drank some of that last night, and I can attest to its unrivaled deliciousness."

Luca rolled his eyes. "Not a wine term."

The two women giggled. "Sorry, we're sort of clueless this way. But we're learning."

"The architect's plan was to build this low into the ground, barely visible from the surrounding area, to preserve the integrity of the natural beauty," he said. "That means most of the structure is actually subterranean, which translates into better temperature control for production and storage of the wines. And the plan was to keep this as green as possible, using local materials such as terra-cotta, oak, weathered steel, and glass."

"The architect did an amazing job," Taylor said. "It's absolutely gorgeous."

"If you look, you'll notice that the design features curves as smooth and natural as a woman's body," he said, pointing toward the exterior of the building. "And all this with a three-story spiral staircase that is itself a work of art and leads to a rooftop restaurant with breathtaking views of the countryside. All in all, a masterful plan."

He led them inside the building, and they descended the staircase to see the cellars. The vaulted cellar conveyed the hushed tones of a cathedral and the intimacy of a church confessional. The terra-cotta walls and honey-wood floors visually warmed the subterranean facilities despite the cool temperatures, and featured cantilevered glass tasting rooms overlooking the barrels.

"I could hang out down here drinking wine all day,"

Larkin said, and Taylor nodded.

"But the upstairs is not to be missed," Luca said. "We'll head there now so you can get a glimpse of the true genius of the place."

As they returned to climb up the remaining flights of steps, they could see what he was talking about.

Patterned light streamed into the building from large circular cuts in the ceiling. The effect was a light-filled contemporary space that included a museum, an event space, an auditorium, a retail shop, and a museum filled with antiques, relics, and artwork from the collections of the twenty-five generations of Romeos who'd preceded Sandro and his siblings.

Taylor could really understand how very connected Sandro was to his past. The Romeos were a clan that was here to stay, and this place was all about paying homage to the family's historic ties to the area. It was hard not to be impressed.

They climbed the steps again to the restaurant rooftop terrace where guests were congregating. White-gloved waitstaff passed gleaming crystal glasses of reserve Chianti to guests, and others passed canapés featuring locally sourced foods such as wild boar, truffles, pecorino cheese, and the celebrated *Cinta Senese* prosciutto.

Taylor and Larkin were busy chatting and enjoying the food, and Taylor didn't even notice Sandro approach.

"Taylor," he said, "I have a few people I'd like you to meet."

Larkin looked at her, confused.

Taylor waved at her dismissively. "Don't worry. I had just wondered where his family was. I guess he's going to introduce me."

It was sort of awkward to be introduced to them now, but she was a guest in their house, so when in Rome...

Taylor's dress dipped low in the front and draped even lower in the back, so when Sandro rested his hand at the base of her spine, she could feel the warmth of his skin on hers, and it made her shudder at the memory of their night.

"My mamma, Fabiana," he said, nodding at a beautifully well-preserved woman of about seventy-five with no-nonsense, short salt-and-pepper hair. She was dressed in a black chiffon dress with sensible shoes. She did not look like the matriarch of a wine empire but rather someone's mother, with a warm smile and an even warmer hug.

"*Cara mia*," she said, hugging her as she kissed each cheek. "We are honored to have you in our home."

Taylor wondered what all she knew of her presence here but hoped it was the bare basics. She didn't even know if anyone was aware of the snake episode, so she kept quiet.

"I'm delighted to meet the wonderful woman who raised such a kind son," Taylor said, laying it on thick. Of course he had been kind to her, so she wasn't lying. She just wasn't talking about those he had been less than kind to.

"And this is my sister, Valentina," Sandro said, pulling her hand gently toward his sister.

Valentina was strikingly beautiful with long, rich, luxuriant black hair and large, coal-black eyes that reminded her of a wet seal.

"Ciao, Taylor," she said, kissing her on both cheeks as well. "So lovely to meet you. My brother has told me so much."

Well, crap. How much could he have told her? Most of

their interactions to date had been pretty X-rated, nothing you'd confide to your sister with.

She looked over at Larkin, who was standing behind Fabiana and mouthing, "He told her all about you?" with a very quizzical look on her face.

Taylor just shrugged. She was getting in too deep.

"I trust my brother is being the perfect gentleman with you," Valentina said, grinning. "If not, just say the word and Mamma and I will straighten him out."

They all laughed at that, and Taylor mentally squirmed because, well, what a lovely family she was never going to see again. She felt like a tease even having a conversation with them at this point.

"He's been nothing but an impeccable host," she said. And freaking amazing in bed, but that won't be an issue down the road, so we just won't go there.

"Please, if we can be of any assistance," Fabiana said. "We want you to feel at home."

Sadly, this place did feel like home. In such a short period of time, it had gone from a stranger's house to a place she could feel like she belonged, snakes and all.

For the first time Taylor noticed a band playing in the background.

Sandro reached out a hand to her. "May I have this dance?"

Well, what was she going to do—shut him down in front of his sweet mamma and little sister?

"Of course," she said, and she extended her hand to his as they walked toward the makeshift dance floor.

It didn't take but a few notes for her to notice the song. "You remembered."

"'Begin the Beguine,'" he said. "How could I forget?"

He pulled her in tightly, and for a minute she was the one who forgot—all about the dark side of Sandro, the part he didn't want her to know about, the stories the Uber driver had told her. And clearly it was true if it was in the gossip magazines. She nestled into the crook of his neck, and his hands settled at the base of her back, so low they were almost cupping her bottom.

He leaned in and whispered in her ear, "Are you ready to tell me what I've done to anger you? Because whatever it is, I'm sure we can work it out. Please. Whatever it is we were starting was really good, Taylor. Please don't let some misunderstanding get in the way of that."

"Can we please not talk about it now? There's really nothing you can do, so let's just enjoy the evening. In fact, I see someone over there I need to talk to, so, well, thanks for the dance."

And before the song even ended, she walked far away from Sandro with no intentions of returning.

Chapter Twenty-Four

SANDRO was vexed by the woman. What could have happened between lunchtime and the start of the party? Absolutely nothing. He'd sent her to the village to pick up Elisabetta, but that was it. He wondered: Elisabetta, would she know something?

He left the terrace and worked his way to the main restaurant level, trying to avoid lengthy conversations as he went, but everyone wanted a piece of him: it was his night. He politely begged out of conversation after conversation till he reached the kitchen, where he pushed open the door and queried several of the catering staff until someone pointed him in the direction of the head chef.

"Ciao, Sandro. You should be out there with your guests, not in here in the hot, messy kitchen." She tugged on his lapel, adding, "You look magnificent."

"*Grazie*, Elisabetta. I was wondering if you might be able to help me with some information. Today I sent Taylor to get you in town. She had my car."

"Oh no, no, no," she said, wagging her finger. "She picked me up with an Uber driver."

"But I gave her the keys to my car." He'd done it as a symbolic act of faith because he knew he had to get past issues with his car after Crazy Gia.

"Maybe she didn't know how to drive it," Elisabetta said. "I know I wouldn't want to take that thing out. It's like driving a jet. Who knows how to do that sort of thing?"

"I didn't even know we could get Uber out here."

"Ah, we have precisely one person driving it in the area," she said. "You remember Liliana, right?"

"Liliana Verducci?"

"No, Liliana Quattrocento," she said. "You should know her. She was friends with that *pazzo* woman you dated."

Pazzo, indeed. Everyone referred to Gia as crazy.

"So Gia's friend Liliana had Taylor's ear for a good twenty minutes before you were with them?"

She shrugged. "I'd say so, yes."

"And what was Taylor like when she arrived?" he said. "Normally she's very outgoing and friendly."

"I'd say she was a little cold, sort of aloof," she said. "Not the warmest of human beings."

He sighed. "*Grazie mille*, Elisabetta. Ciao, ciao."

He turned and returned to face the hordes, hoping to find Taylor somewhere amidst the over five hundred guests who by now had congregated in the place. He had to set her straight.

Taylor was working the crowd hard, handing out business cards and giving her usual elevator pitch to anyone she recognized from the guest list, which she'd studied

earlier in the day. She hated to admit the men were far easier to persuade than the women. Not that women weren't supportive of one another, but perhaps just women in this crowd weren't keen on parting with their—or their husband's—wealth. Which was a shame because the place was not lacking in one-of-a-kind couture fashions. She knew because she'd worn some of them in last season's fashion shows in Milan and Paris.

One particularly flinty-eyed dowager glared Taylor down as she tried to appeal to the woman's gasbag of a husband.

"Yes, of course it's tax deductible," Taylor said. I can send you brochures with more information if you're willing to commit fifty thousand." She used to hate hitting people up for money, but she knew these people could well afford it and wouldn't even notice the money missing from their bank accounts.

An hour later, she was back down in the cellars. Most people seemed to be congregating upstairs, especially as it was a lovely evening out. But she was looking for an American hedge fund manager she had been told would be down here who had crested the billionaire threshold ages ago. Surely he could pony up some money for her cause.

She wandered through the casks, first relatively crowded with people, then she turned toward another room with casks from the reserve Chianti she had enjoyed so much, and there in a far corner was the man, Edgar Whittington. She'd heard he was pompous, loved to be told how marvelous he was, with an ego that exceeded his bank account totals even.

"Ah, Mr. Whittington," she said. "So lovely to see you here."

He eyed her up and down like a woman on a thousand-calorie-a-day diet would a slice of pie. His large belly betrayed his fondness for excess in food and drink. He kept dabbing his sweaty face with a cocktail napkin. She was going to have to make this quick.

"Even lovelier to see you," he said, moving closer to her and wrapping his arm around her shoulder.

"Mr. Whittington, sir," she said. "I was hoping I could put you down for a contribution to my charity, Rags to Riches. We help provide clothes for children in poverty who can't afford them."

He lifted a brow and lowered his hand so that it was tucked beneath her arm, encroaching toward her breast. She squirmed to shift his grip farther away. He was downright vile. But she wanted his money.

"Well, if they can't afford them, maybe they should find a job to help pay for them," he said. "Teach a man to fish."

Taylor wrinkled her brow. "But they're children, sir."

"And what better time to learn the benefits of a hard day's work? Start 'em young, maybe then you keep them off the public dole." He placed his hand back where it had been and literally slipped it beneath the metallic bodice of her halter dress.

She swatted his hand away. She so wanted to slug the man for his arrogance. What a bastard. "Huh. Isn't it true that you made your first fortune in big agriculture?"

"As a matter of fact, I did. Seeds, pesticides, all sorts of chemicals. The whole world uses them now. They have no choice in the matter." He gave her an exaggerated wink.

"And isn't it true that big ag is one of the biggest benefactors of corporate welfare? Far, far more than poor

children in an inner city might get."

"I'm not sure where you get your information from, but I'm a hardworking individual who earned my money through blood, sweat, and toil."

"Funny," she said, turning to face him. "I thought it came from seed money from your wealthy father."

He smiled an oily smile, the type you might see from a deranged killer before he plunged a knife in. "Why don't you cut to the chase, Miss McFarland." He reached out with his pointer finger and slowly dragged it down along the outline of her breast. "I've got something you want, and you've got something I want. So let's talk about how we're both going to end up happy." He slipped his fingers beneath the inside edge of her gown, and she was prepared to wind up and hit him.

"I beg your pardon," she heard a voice from behind her say. "Exactly what are you doing here?"

She turned her head to see Sandro walking toward them. He glanced down to see Whittington's fingers moving along her breast, and he reacted on impulse, coldcocking him just as Taylor reared up and kicked him in the balls. Doubled over in pain, Whittington staggered backward into the hard terra-cotta wall.

"Sandro," Taylor said, her voice shaking. "Oh, that was just awful." Tears sprang from her eyes as she looked back and forth between the two men. "And I can't decide who is worse between the two of you. All I know is I'm disgusted with men. You're both horrid."

With that she stormed off, sobbing.

Chapter Twenty-Five

SERIOUSLY, he saved her from some son of a bitch who was so rich and so used to getting what he wanted that he didn't think twice before forcing himself on a woman who wanted nothing to do with him, and instead of thanking him, she accused him of being equally repugnant and fled the place. He almost wondered if Taylor had a twin, like a really demented one, and she had replaced the sweet Taylor he'd made love to that morning. He couldn't make sense of the transition that had occurred.

In the meantime, his knuckles hurt from hitting the asshole, and he had a guest—soon to be ex-guest—crumpled and bleeding on the floor. He reached for a walkie-talkie in his pocket and summoned a bodyguard.

"Giovanni, I need you to get rid of the vermin that has apparently infested my pristine cellars," he said. "You'll find him curled up on the floor, looking for his lost nuts. Be sure to show him outside the gate and let the police know he's not allowed to intrude."

Sandro kicked Whittington aside as he left, closing the door off to keep guests from wandering in until Giovanni took care of things.

For a day that started out near perfect, things had certainly taken a precipitous turn for the worse. He looked at his watch. Dammit. He needed to be upstairs to make a speech and a toast in minutes. He'd have to pursue Taylor afterward and hope she was still on the premises. Knowing her, she'd be on the first flight out. But family obligations

came first.

As he approached the stage set up for him to address the crowd, he saw Luca and Larkin dancing. He glanced over the nearby railing to see a woman in a familiar metallic silver evening gown racing from the building toward the palazzo.

He grabbed Luca's shoulder and the couple stopped dancing. "Dude, I need your help. It's Taylor."

"Ohmygod, is she all right?" Larkin said.

He nodded toward the shiny figure below.

"Wait a minute. Isn't that Taylor?" she said, pointing at her friend's diminishing figure. "Where's she running to? What is going on? I don't know what's gotten into her, but she took a turn toward the strange sometime this afternoon. And now it looks like she's fleeing a fire."

"It's a long story," Sandro said. "But I need you to stop her please."

Luca and Larkin looked at each other. "Uh, if you say so, *mio cugino*," Luca said to his cousin. "But I'm starting to wonder if you've got some issues you might need to talk out with a specialist."

Sandro softly smacked his hand upside the back of Luca's head. "I don't need a shrink. I need that woman. Now."

Taylor was so confused. Just completely off center and couldn't figure out quite how to right herself. In a few short days, she'd gone from strongly disliking Sandro to craving the next moment she could be alone with the man to detesting the very ground he walked on. Then he went and did something chivalrous when that scummy man was assaulting her—even though she was perfectly capable of handling herself, but still. It was so sweet of him. Nevertheless, that simply meant he was a sweet man who could be a coldhearted bastard. He could get in line behind plenty of those types. And those types were not for her.

She'd fled the building so fast—only taking time to peel off her silver Stuart Weitzman stiletto sandals so she didn't break an ankle—she hadn't even had a chance to look back. Now she was pacing in the garden near the pool. She could hear the faint sounds of music and the din of hundreds of conversations drifting toward her in the night air. It was a lovely party, but no way could she have remained there under the circumstances. She felt bad; Sandro's mother and sister seemed so sweet. They'd think her terribly rude when they learned she'd left without even saying good-bye or thanking them. But what else could she do?

The garden at least was soothing to her: so full of color, including one of her favorite flowers, lantana shrubs, which edged the garden with their multicolored buds alongside fat purple allium. The scent of thyme, rosemary, and sage wafted skyward with the light breeze. The smells of Tuscany were intoxicating and oddly soothing despite her feeling off-the-charts stressed. She felt so connected to this place; it was a shame that she would be forever removed from it in just a few short hours.

Taylor strolled toward a large marble fountain that expelled water through the mouths of three large carp. She stood by the fountain staring at them, thinking she, too, was really just a fish out of water here. She didn't belong here; it was Sandro's home. Perhaps his hospitality was such that she felt she somehow belonged. But that was all a false construct, just like the personality attributes she had given him. He might have seemed like a nice man, but a nice man doesn't leave a woman at the altar.

Lost in thought, she didn't even hear Larkin calling her name until she came staggering toward her.

"Christ, woman," she said. "You've got me all sweaty and hot and gasping for air trying to get ahold of you before you do something crazy."

Taylor looked at her and squinted her eyes. "What are you talking about, doing something crazy?"

"I don't know," Larkin said. "All I know is Luca and I were having a fine time, enjoying the evening, dancing on the terrace, when Sandro rushed over to us, pointed to you running at warp speed away from the place, and said he needed you. Which, by the way, is so romantic."

Taylor turned and walked away from her friend. "Are you kidding me? Romantic? Sandro? About as romantic as a slap in the face."

Larkin stared at her. "Okay, then…," she said, biting her lip. "Would you mind catching me up to speed on what the hell's been going on since you have apparently completely lost your shit?"

"I have lost no such thing!"

"Well, what is going on with you?" she said. "We get here, you and Sandro clearly do not hit it off. Then you do hit it off, then you don't, then you do. This afternoon you

Jenny Gardiner

seemed so fine, then you get back from your errand and you've morphed into 'hormone woman' or something. I thought you and I were friends, Taylor. The least you could do is explain to me what is going on."

Chapter Twenty-Six

TAYLOR took a seat on the wide marble steps that were flanked by two large urns that were overflowing with cascading flowers. She rested her elbows on her knees, leaned forward, and proceeded to tell her friend everything: the snake, the early morning sex, the Uber ride with Liliana, the hedge fund guy she kicked in the balls, the whole spiel.

"Wow," Larkin said. "You sure do lead an interesting life, I'll tell you."

Taylor rolled her eyes. "Interesting at times maybe. But right now I'd say more like disappointing."

"Okay, so I don't know all the details about Sandro, but I have to believe he's a good man. Why would Luca have spent his life as his best friend if he weren't?"

"Uh, because they're related to each other?"

"Just because you've got a blood connection doesn't mean you have to care about someone, let alone take them into your heart."

Taylor leaned back, resting her palms on the marble steps on either side of her.

"I don't know. I don't know. I just don't know." She kept shaking her head.

"Don't you think you at least owe Sandro the chance to explain his side of things? Rather than relying on rumors and innuendo, and instead running away and leaving everyone confused and hurt?"

"Look, Larkin, I appreciate your concern, but really, I don't need your assistance. I left the party because I couldn't take it anymore. I needed to get away from Sandro. It was too hard for me to wrestle with these different sides to that man. But I know he's bad, and he's certainly bad for me."

"Bad?" she heard a man's voice approaching. Luca.

Oh, great. Here comes the cavalry.

"Yeah," Taylor said. "I know everything about the pregnant woman he left at the altar. And I don't know how anyone could be so cavalier. What a jerk."

Luca scratched his head, and Larkin looked like she was listening to someone speaking Portuguese.

"Pregnant woman? Altar?" Luca said. "I'm not sure I have a clue what you're talking about."

"Uh, his fiancée? Gia? The one he dumped, and then he called the police on her even though he was the one who was wrong."

"Seriously, Taylor, I don't know who's been talking to you, but you are talking out of your ass," he said. "Sandro was never engaged to anybody, let alone Gia Sandretti. And she certainly wasn't pregnant with his child. Gia was a crazy, hot-tempered stalker who basically ruined the past year of Sandro's life."

Taylor knit her brows. "What are you talking about? I heard the whole story just today, from someone who knows Gia well."

"And who would you choose to believe, Taylor? A complete stranger who claims to know the true story? Or the man who's been victimized by Gia and her cohorts for months and months now?"

"Victimized?"

"Uh, yeah," Luca said. "Gia was a jealous freak who convinced herself that Sandro—the man who is loyal as an

old dog, I might add—was cheating on him. She spied on his e-mails, his text messages, she called numbers in his cell phone to check up on him. She became so enraged with him about a supposed affair he wasn't even having that she threw her shoe at him, causing him to have to get stitches when the heel sliced his arm.

"Sandro tried to ease away from her gently, but she dug in and made things worse for him. He got to the point he was afraid to leave the house because he thought she might try to run him off the road. And then finally she drove up here in broad daylight, poured gasoline all over his Lamborghini, and lit it on fire."

Taylor could feel the rush of heat to her face with the sense of shame she felt, having never even questioned what she'd learned.

"And the thing is, Taylor, I thought you of all people would at least ask me before judging me like that," said a voice behind her.

She turned to see Sandro standing there. She shook her head, confused, embarrassed, overwhelmed, exhausted. "I don't know what to think about any of this. I just need to leave here."

With that she picked up her sandals and raced up the steps to the terrace and into the house.

Taylor was normally so cautious with her clothes. She of all people knew what a precious commodity they could be, and she was careful to handle hers so that they would last. But now, instead, she tossed things into her suitcase as quickly as she could find her belongings, scattered as they were throughout the room. Funny how she no longer even thought about lurking snakes; instead, she knew she just wanted to get away from that one snake who had gotten under her skin.

She heard a soft knock on the door and chose to ignore it, hoping whoever it was would go away.

Of course the knock got louder, dammit.

She found her toiletry bag and began tossing her things in there. She pulled her shampoo and other toiletries out of the shower and threw them in as well. Normally she'd bag everything so it wouldn't leak in transit, but there was no time for that now. She just wanted to get out of there as quickly as humanly possible.

She came out of the bathroom to find Sandro sitting on the bed, his back up against the headboard. Which was fine by her because she was no longer going to be sleeping there anyhow, so he could sit there all night as far as she was concerned. It was his bed anyway, when it came down to it. She remembered when she slept in here that first night, she'd been so tempted to draw the blue velvet canopy closed around the bed just to feel secure, not to mention a little regal. But now she was just going to keep throwing things into her suitcase and avoid further discussions with Sandro.

"We've got nothing to say to each other," she said to him, throwing her yoga pants and shirt into her bag. She wished she'd changed out of this damned silver gown, but

now she was stuck in it as long as he loomed before her.

"Denial can afford a lot of protection from the truth."

"I'm not denying anything," she said, which in itself was a denial. *Damn, he had her there.*

"I understand you had a little talk with Liliana this afternoon." He crossed his arms. "You might not realize this, but Liliana is Gia's best friend."

Taylor shrugged. It wasn't her business who any of those women were. She tossed her panties into the bag one by one, maybe just to make Sandro see what he'd be missing out on. It was stupid of her, of course. But she might even admit she wasn't behaving particularly rationally.

"After I finally got rid of Gia once and for all—or so I thought until I realized she has her emissaries still trying to do her bidding—I struggled with trusting women again. I mean this woman not only hurt me physically, but she destroyed my five-hundred-thousand-euro car. Because she was jealous! Of nothing and no one!" he said. "Deep down, I knew she was a crazy woman and really needed mental health treatment. But I knew, too, that there was nothing I could do to help her, and the best I could do was get the woman out of my life with as little fallout as possible."

Taylor remained tight-lipped as she closed her suitcase and clamped the locks shut.

"When you showed up, I was in no frame of mind to deal with a woman," he said. "It's why I made sure to keep you at arm's length. When you arrived that night, absolutely luminous and effervescent, I just didn't know what to make of the feelings you triggered in me. Instantly I felt drawn to you, but of course I was worried I was a moth being drawn to the flame again. And I vowed never to put myself in that situation again. Not only could my mind and heart not handle it, but also I couldn't subject my family to the potential repercussions of being linked with someone as dangerous as Gia. Not that you were dangerous, but I no longer trusted myself to make good decisions when it came to women."

"So you assumed I was a crazy person then?" she said, leaning against the bedpost and crossing her arms and legs, sending a message to him through her body language: *closed for business.*

"No," he said. "I just couldn't trust. I couldn't trust myself or anyone else for that matter. Which was why it was so inconvenient that you kept insinuating your way into my heart. That first night you were so wounded… I wanted badly to be that man who could protect you. It brought out all the caveman feelings I'd suppressed after Gia. But you seemed so fragile and vulnerable, and I knew I could help you."

She allowed herself to smile, thinking about the unexpected turn of events that night.

"And then, well, things happened fast," he said. "And suddenly they stopped just as quickly as they'd heated up. I'd be lying if I said I wasn't upset about that. I mean, I'm a man. You can't leave a man hanging on the edge like that without instilling at least some sense of resentment.

"At first I managed to successfully keep my distance, but dammit, you kept sneaking back into my psyche. All those stories of your generosity and kindness of heart. It was more than I could bear. And then the damned snake."

She stepped away from the bedpost, looking over her shoulder, suddenly remembering the potential for snakes. She rubbed her hands against her arms, reminding herself

there was no snake lurking in here.

"When I came back and found you in my bed, I didn't know whether that was the greatest gift ever or just the worst tease imaginable," he said. "I wanted nothing more than to pick up where we'd left off, but I didn't dare for fear of repercussions. I couldn't just help myself even if you were sleeping in my bed."

She smiled. "I mean, I sort of had to. No way could I have slept in here with snakes roaming freely and all."

He rolled his eyes. "Yes, our home is a veritable herpetarium. Admit it: you wanted me as much as I wanted you."

She pursed her lips. "Well, I did have some regrets about how things ended that first night. It probably wasn't very fair of me to leave you high and dry like I did."

He nodded. "I agree. Left me to my own devices. Which I suppose was where I already was anyhow, having sworn off women for a while."

Her eyes opened wide. "Seriously? You took care of yourself after you left here?"

He frowned. "What else was I going to do? Contrary to Gia's beliefs, I don't harbor a harem of women to service me at my every whim."

Tired of standing, Taylor came over and sat down on the edge of the bed, keeping a safe enough distance from Sandro, mostly because she didn't trust herself around him. He was doing a good job of chipping away at her anger.

"But by then I'd grown unfortunately rather fond of my little ice princess," he said. "And when I got the chance to fall asleep at least in the same bed as you, well, how could I say no?"

"At some point you decided I was fair game, because I

woke up with you draped over my body."

"I'm afraid I can't take responsibility for things I do in my sleep," he said, grinning. "But imagine my delight to wake up with my hand strategically placed on your breast. It was like winning the World Cup and the Olympics without having even trained for them."

She let out a laugh. "That's quite a prize then."

He reached for her hand and pulled her toward him. "The most amazing prize I've ever been awarded."

"Which is saying something, considering your many wine-making prizes."

"You know it," he said, laughing. "Do you know, Taylor, that I gave you the keys to my car because it was a part of me letting go of my anger and mistrust? I know it was an invisible gesture to you, but to me, it let me know I could trust again."

She opened her eyes wide. "I wish you'd have clued me in to that. Because when I went out there and saw you'd given me the keys to a veritable Lear jet… Well, there was no way I was going to be responsible for taking that thing out onto actual roads. With hazards, and cars, and wild boar that could run out in front of the car."

He laughed. "Wild boar? Since when have you encountered wild boar anywhere but on your dinner plate?"

"Since when have you encountered venomous snakes in your guests' bedrooms?"

He aimed a finger at her. "You've got a good point." Still holding one hand, he pulled Taylor even closer in with the other so they were pressed up against each other. "Please tell me you believe me when I say I never did anything to hurt Gia. And more importantly that I would never do anything to hurt you."

She nodded. "It's been weird. All these conflicting feelings and emotions, and then I was socked with this story that made you out to be such an ogre. Maybe I thought all along you were too good to be true, and then Liliana's words reinforced my fears. I don't know. But I'm really sorry, Sandro. And to make matters worse, all this on your big day. You've got five hundred of your closest friends waiting for you to rejoin them at your party."

"Make that four hundred and ninety-eight."

"Ninety-eight?"

He nodded. "Of course. We're now missing that creep Edgar Whittington, which takes it to four ninety-nine. And of course your absence, the most important of them all, brings it down to four hundred and ninety-eight."

"Please don't miss out on the party on my account."

He leaned over and pressed his lips to her, stroking her hair with his hands. "I'm perfectly happy with the party we've got going here." He slid his hand into the deep vee in the front of her dress and cupped her breast.

"You know this was all your fault," she said. "If you hadn't presumed I wanted to drive that awful, scary car of yours, this huge misunderstanding wouldn't have happened."

"I thought you'd be excited to drive it," he said. "The pulse of the engine, the grip on the road, the thrill of the chase."

"Trust me, the chase doesn't do it for me. Besides, you should know I have issues with cars," she said, smiling against his mouth. "In fact, from here on out, I will gladly let you do all the driving. But the most important thing you need to drive are the snakes, out of this house!"

"Are you crazy?" he said, glad that she was not even

remotely so. "I owe that snake a debt of gratitude. I might just have to assign him his own room."

She playfully smacked him as she reached to draw the velvet curtains around the bed closed. "Shut up and kiss me, Alessandro Romeo. We've got a party to return to. As soon as we finish up our little party for two."

And they did return to the party, a bit disheveled but happy. Taylor, of course, had never felt happier, finally feeling she'd found a place where her roots could grow deep.

Thank you so much for reading *Red-Hot Romeo!* I hope you enjoyed it! If so, please help others find this book:

1. Help other people find this book by writing a review.

2. Sign up for my new releases email so you can find out about the next book as soon as it's available and get fun giveaways.
   http://eepurl.com/baaewn

3. Like my Facebook page.
   www.facebook.com/jennygardinerbooks

And I love to hear from readers! Let me know what you think about my books! You can write to me at jenny@jennygardiner.net, and visit me on the web at www.jennygardiner.net.

Turn the page for a sneak peek of the next book in The Royal Romeos – **Black Sheep Romeo**!

Black Sheep Romeo

Chapter One

FREE-SPIRITED wanderer Lizzie Moretti liked nothing better than to up and move on, which was ironic, considering for the past couple of years, all of her efforts had gone toward putting down roots. Only those were of the plant variety, and by the time they germinated and took hold in the rich soil, usually she was long gone and on to the next farm. Lizzie—Lizard, to her friends—never stayed in one place for very long, and that was fine by her. She loved to see the world and had traveled extensively, usually working on farms in exchange for room and board.

In recent years, she'd planted coffee beans in Indonesia, rice in Bangladesh, hops in Germany, and now grapes in Italy—although here she'd not plant but instead help the intensive efforts to pick grapes at their peak of ripeness with the impending harvest. She loved the idea of learning how to make wine, and had hoped while there to spend a little time looking into her own Italian heritage, as her father's grandparents had emigrated from Italy to America at the turn of the last century. Maybe that's where her wandering came from. No doubt about it, she lived a nomad's life, but it suited her. But perhaps a lengthy stay in

Italy would be a nice way to spend the autumn.

Growing up in a military family, she'd learned the hard way not to get too comfortable in a place, never establishing her own roots, because inevitably her family was displaced each time her father got assigned to yet another military base, which gave them virtually no time to pack and go, and left little chance even for farewells. Not that she was one for long goodbyes anyhow: it was too painful to make good friends because it was too hurtful to then watch them in the rear-view mirror as her mom drove down the street yet again en route to a new destination—her father having already moved to his newest posting.

So she learned to appreciate each new place, to live with wings on her feet, always at the ready to take off on a moment's notice. As a young adult, she'd grown to love this transient existence, with little more than a pack on her back and a pair of Teva sandals on her feet. It made it hard to collect mementos of her travels—after all, there was no place to store them in a forty-pound backpack. Besides, where on earth would she ever put them? Her father had died from a roadside bomb in the Anbar Province of Iraq more than a decade ago, and her mother had remarried and moved on with yet another military man, leaving no true home to which Lizzie could even return, if and when she ever chose.

Besides, her lifestyle kept things light and carefree, and gave her the chance to follow her impulses, and—more importantly—trust her instincts, which so far hadn't steered her wrong. She'd arrived at a small farm in the Chianti region of Tuscany only a few days ago, hoping to work the grape harvest, then stick around to harvest the olives several weeks later. She'd heard it was a lot of fun—despite being hard work—and she was excited to experience the lush, green countryside of central Italy, the land of fabulous food and wine.

She'd organized the job online, and the host farmer was responsible to ensuring she was legal to participate in the harvest, a coveted job often left only to experts and family members at the large vineyards. But this place was supposedly small, so the opportunity presented itself to her. Lizzie's plan was to stick around for maybe six weeks, then perhaps work her way toward Australia or New Zealand just in time for the antipodean summertime, maybe find a coastal area, some sun, sand, and a new land and people to discover.

She was a bit disappointed that this vineyard had no other fellow travelers like herself to work the harvest, though. She'd arrived two days ago to learn that the sleeping accommodations were primitive at best: a stone shed with no heat, and judging from the scratching and squeaking sounds she'd heard at night, plenty of mice as unwanted roommates. The bathroom was in another shed she had to walk to in the middle of the night and featured a stinky, rudimentary composting toilet.

Alas, it seemed this wasn't going to be a holiday in Tuscany that would involve long, filling lunches followed by exploring the countryside. Not that she'd expected as much, but a girl could dream, right? She had, however, hoped to be able to wander the region a bit. Her host, an older, grizzled, surly Italian man named Luigi Scalfone, had stated in their email exchange that there would be transportation, but that turned out to be a rusty, decrepit bike with two flat tires. So far the meals promised her hadn't met basic standards either: they were mostly composed of half-ripened season-end tomatoes that he himself rejected, along with the rotting unsellable vegetables left over from the fields, paired with tins of tuna fish. Even for breakfast. It would be a test of Lizzie's stamina—and stubborn streak—toughing it out for six weeks at this rate. Clearly this agreement wasn't to be a cultural exchange as she'd hoped, but rather a one-sided labor exploitation on Luigi's part.

Over the past few years she'd had mixed experiences wherever she settled in temporarily, but most often things worked out well. Occasionally another farm hand was disagreeable. Sometimes the job description didn't live up to expectations. But for the first time since she'd started as an itinerant helper, she had a bad feeling. First off Luigi was clearly drunk when she arrived just before dusk on that first evening. She'd hopped off a bus about three miles away and walked the rest of the distance, her heavy pack weighing her down, but the walk doing her good.

She'd passed a gorgeous, very large vineyard, anchored by a massive manor home, on her way to her destination, and half-wondered what it would be like to work there instead. It was so beautiful—and sprawling-—from what she could see from a distance. Maybe if she volunteered there as a guest worker she could sleep like a princess on six-hundred thread-count sheets and after a few hours toiling in the fields, take some time to lounge poolside, or better yet float the afternoon away on a raft, admiring the rolling hillside, peppered with olive groves and vineyards as far as the eye could see. As if. Lizzie could hardly fathom that lifestyle, but she enjoyed the fantasy while her feet hit the pavement, en route to *Fattoria Luigi*.

When she arrived at the vineyard, she was met by the

namesake himself, slurring his words and occupying her personal space, his alcohol-laced breath hot and strong beneath her nose, in a manner that made her feel most uncomfortable. He spoke few words, ushered her to the less-than-plush accommodations, and left her to figure out dinner on her own when he passed out on his bed.

"Welcome to Tuscany," Lizzie muttered as she scrounged in the tiny kitchen for some pasta. She fixed a serving of plain noodles before retiring to the privacy of the small hovel she would call home for the next several weeks.

For the first couple of days, she was assigned particularly menial work: sweeping the house, washing dishes, moving wheelbarrows full of rocks, and mucking donkey stalls. Though she was supposed to be working the grape harvest, she was perfectly happy to help out where needed. But she felt terribly unwelcome around her host, who mostly grunted and snapped out short commands to her while he drank until he again passed out.

Clearly this wasn't going to be one of her favorite destinations, the way things were shaping up so far. She held out hope that other workers would soon show up to lighten the mood of the place, but so far none. On the third evening, Lizzie took a look at herself in the muted reflection of one of the stainless steel wine tanks in the fermentation room. She had looked better.

Understatement of the year, she thought.

Her large, damp brown eyes poked out from a dirt-encrusted face. Her hair looked like it was going in the direction of Bob Marley. If she didn't wash it she'd have dreadlocks by the end of the week. Using what little warm water was afforded her in the outhouse, Lizzie washed her face, scrubbed her long, dark brown hair, then plaited it into two pigtail braids, and tucked herself in for bed, ready for a good night's sleep.

Soon after she'd lapsed, exhausted, into a deep slumber, she felt the press of a large body against her back. She turned her head and in the darkness made out the grizzled face of her drunken host, whose obvious arousal was insinuating itself into the cushion of her backside. Terrified, she knew she couldn't even scream for help; there was no one here but the two of them, save but a host of mice who would be of no help.

Fortunately, Lizzie had learned long ago to be prepared, so she never went to bed without her minimal belongings together in one place. Thinking quickly, she thrust her elbow hard into his solar plexus, rolled immediately out of bed, grabbed her pack and her boots, and took off before Luigi had a chance to regain his breath, writhing as he was in a drunken stupor. She felt no pity for the man as she rushed out the rickety shed door, shutting it tightly behind her.

As soon as she was past the sight line of the house, Lizzie stopped to put on her hiking boots, secured her pack onto her back, and quickened her pace to get well beyond the fattoria before her disgusting, drunken host could ever catch up with her. Sure Lizzie liked to move on at will, but usually it was when she was good and ready, not because she was nearly assaulted. She'd had some squeamish experiences occasionally while traveling as what was essentially a migrant worker, but never had she felt personally violated.

Once she reached the road, she decided to turn right and follow her tracks the way she'd arrived here days

earlier, knowing there would be at least be other farms and vineyards along the way. Perhaps a car would pass and she could hitch a ride somewhere—anywhere—just to get some distance between her and the creepy farmer. Before she could even think about being comfortable, she needed to keep herself safe. The last thing she'd expected to have to worry about in the welcoming hills of Tuscany.

Chapter Two

MATTEO Romeo had arrived back at his family's vineyard just in time for the grape harvest. After a year away from his mother and siblings and the burdensome familial obligations he wasn't sure he wanted to accept as his own, he knew at the very least he had to return for the *vendemmia*, the annual grape harvest that all of Italy anticipates as much as a child would the arrival of Santa on Christmas morning.

And even though Matteo had felt a downright dire need to get away from the disapproving eyes of his mother and his older brother Sandro—who made him feel like a failure for not wanting to carry on with the family name as expected—there was an inexplicable magnetic pull back to Chianti at this time of year, despite his determination to stay away. Yet he was conflicted, because when it came down to it, Sandro was the oldest of the five Romeo siblings, and *Cantine dei Marchesi Romeo* was ultimately going to land in his hands, so why should Matteo put too much of his own blood, sweat and tears into it?

He asked himself that, but in fact he knew the real reason he'd flown the nest was because of his propensity to scandalize: be it his mother, his brother, or even the residents of the nearby small, ancestral town of Santa Romeo. They expected Matteo to carry on responsibly and uphold the family name at all times, and so when he supposedly got a local girl pregnant, everyone was outraged. Even though ultimately it was he who was indignant, because the baby turned out not to be his. As he'd suspected, his one-off fling with the young woman wasn't what "took", but rather the many nights of her sleeping with the married husband of a local schoolteacher had.

Matteo didn't really think he deserved to be lumped into the scandal between the lot of them; he'd just had sex with her after the town *festa* celebrating last year's grape harvest. One time. And sure, once was all it took, he knew that. But eventually he realized she was much further along than the timeline that would have pegged him as the baby daddy, and once he realized that and coerced a confession from the woman, he decided it was time to put some distance between him and this suffocating one-horse town that had owned him his entire life.

He wasn't sure when he'd return back to the ancestral fold, and surprised even himself when the yearning for that sense of belonging that only came from family and *terroir* began to stir deep within him. He'd spent the past year of his life wandering; he was lucky he had the unlimited funds to do this. And he did it with a vengeance, traveling first class to the far reaches of the world, first China, then Thailand, next to Africa, eventually to Central and South America. He'd enjoyed himself immensely, staying at top-tier hotels and bedding down beautiful women in every port along the way. But with the vendemmia looming, his heart was calling him back home, despite himself.

He arrived days before the harvest was to begin, just in time for a huge family Sunday lunch.

"The prodigal son!" his sister Valentina squealed, running to embrace him when she saw him drop his bags on the terrace where a long table was set for the meal. "I knew you'd come home for the harvest. I just knew you couldn't stay away from your favorite sister."

Matteo stood back to take a good, long look at his younger sister. "Don't you mean my only sister?" he said with a grin. "Ahhh, Valentina. It's hard to imagine how it's possible, but you've gotten even more beautiful in my absence. I've come back to keep the men away from you." He kissed her cheeks.

She waved him away. "Don't you dare keep them away from me. I need all the help I can get to attract them. Mamma," she called to her mother, who was inside putting the finishing touches on the meal. "You'll never guess what the cat dragged in."

"I hope it's not another snake," his mother Fabiana said, looking up as she walked onto the terrace. As soon as she saw her son, she wiped her hands on her dress and ran to him. "Matteo! *Finalemente.* Finally you have returned home." She kissed his cheeks and hugged him fiercely.

"Mamma," he said, inhaling the aroma from platters of food being placed on the table by staff. "I couldn't stay away from your cooking." He rubbed his belly.

"I knew I could lure you home, my sweet boy," she said, kissing him again. "Sit, eat."

"Did you just call for your sweet boy?" Matteo's brother Sandro came out to the terrace, only to see Matteo being smothered with hugs from their mother.

"Look who's come home!" Fabiana said.

Sandro stared at his brother, finally giving a short nod. "Matteo."

The two of them could almost be twins, both in age and appearance. Both had wavy dark hair, Matteo's a little shorter, and their mother's warm, brown eyes. Sandro had a moustache and goatee, providing the distinguishing factor between the two.

Matteo nodded back. "Sandro."

The last thing Matteo had wanted was an immediate stand-off with his brother. They'd long been good friends, though they parted ways when it came to family expectations, which was why Matteo left in the first place.

The two men looked at each other for a brief moment until the standoff was broken by a gorgeous tall, blonde with an unmistakable American accent.

"It's about time," his brother's girlfriend said, Taylor McFarland. "I was beginning to think it was something I'd said!" She enveloped him in a hug, then remembered she forgot the obligatory cheek kisses so threw them in for good measure. It wasn't long after Taylor had taken up with Sandro that Matteo and his brother had their falling out and Matteo had fled.

"Taylor, you look as magnificent as ever," Matteo said. "I don't know why you put up with my brother, when you could have me instead."

She laughed. "Thanks, but I like the hardship cases. More of a challenge."

"You've got a challenge with Sandro, no doubt," he said, shaking his head.

"Everyone, sit," Fabiana said as they sat down to their feast. "Sandro, pour the wine. Lorenzo, Francesco and Giorgio are coming late for lunch today. It will be perfect to have all of my children together at last. What a way to start the vendemmia."

Matteo looked at his family members who were already gathered around the table, happy to see them, yet apprehensive after being away for so long, wondering

where he would fit in once he'd stepped even further away from the fold. What a way to start the vendemmia, indeed.

Black Sheep Romeo
coming December 6, 2016.

All books by Jenny Gardiner:

Contemporary Romances
The Royal Romeos
Book 1: Red Hot Romeo
Book 2: Black Sheep Romeo

It's Reigning Men series:
Book 1: Something in the Heir
Book 2: Heir Today, Gone Tomorrow
Book 3: Bad to the Throne
Book 4: Love is in the Heir
Book 5: Shame of Thrones
Book 6: Throne for a Loop
Book 7: It's Getting Hot in Heir
Book 8: A Court Gesture

Other Contemporary Romances:
Accidentally on Purpose
Compromising Positions

Single Titles:
Slim to None
Anywhere but Here
Sleeping with Ward Cleaver
Where the Heart Is

Jenny Gardiner

Memoir:
Bite Me: A Parrot, A Family and a Whole Lot of
Flesh Wounds

Essay Anthology:
Naked Man on Main Street

Thank you again for your ongoing support!

Jenny Gardiner

About the Author

Jenny Gardiner is the author of #1 Kindle Bestseller *Slim to None* and the award-winning novel *Sleeping with Ward Cleaver*. Her latest works are the *It's Reigning Men* series, featuring *Something in the Heir, Heir Today Gone Tomorrow, Bad to the Throne; Love is in the Heir, Shame of Thrones; Throne for a Loop; It's Getting Hot in Heir; A Court Gesture;* and her new Royal Romeos series, featuring *Red-Hot Romeo* and the upcoming *Black Sheep Romeo* She also published the memoir *Winging It: A Memoir of Caring for a Vengeful Parrot Who's Determined to Kill Me,* now re-titled *Bite Me: a Parrot, a Family and a Whole Lot of Flesh Wounds;* the novels *Anywhere but Here; Where the Heart Is;* the essay collection *Naked Man on Main Street*, and *Accidentally on Purpose* and *Compromising Positions* (writing as Erin Delany); and is a contributor to the humorous dog anthology *I'm Not the Biggest Bitch in This Relationship*.

Her work has been found in Ladies Home Journal, the Washington Post, Marie-Claire.com, and on NPR's Day to Day. She was also a columnist for Charlottesville's Daily Progress for over a decade, and is the Volunteer Coordinator for the Virginia Film Festival.

She has worked as a professional photographer, an orthodontic assistant (learning quite readily that she was not cut out for a career in polyester), a waitress (probably her highest-paying job), a TV reporter, a pre-obituary writer, as well as a publicist to a United States Senator (where she first learned to write fiction). She's photographed Prince Charles (and her assistant husband got him to chuckle!), Elizabeth Taylor, and the president of Uganda. She and her family and menagerie of pets now live a less exotic life in Virginia.

Visit Jenny at her website and sign up for her newsletter, her blog, or find her on Facebook and Twitter. And every blue moon she'll post adorable pictures of her pets on Instagram as @thejennygardiner.

www.ingramcontent.com/pod-product-compliance
Lightning Source LLC
Chambersburg PA
CBHW071248130626
46556CB00003B/1211